It has to get better

Yasmin Curtis

Edited by RJ Locksley

Cover design by Amber Curtis

Formatting by Dawn Black

ISBN: 978-1-3999-5520-1

This is for all of the girls who can't see a way out. For all of the girls who try to be fiercely independent. For all of the girls who struggle to hide their inner sass. For all of the girls who want more.

This is a work of fiction. Names, characters, places and incidents are either the product of the author's imagination or are used fictitiously. Any resemblance to actual persons, living or dead, events, or locales is entirely coincidental.

Please see the trigger warnings in the book description ahead of reading.

Contents

CHAPTER 1

I'm Fine

Rosie

I dragged my tired feet onto the rustic ferry as a few cars inched their way through the relentless rain. Stuffing my change and ticket back into my pocket, I hurried over to a makeshift shelter nailed to the structure of the wheelhouse, juggling my bag and my dog in my arms.

I slid down against the wall, my legs crossed in front of me with my dachshund nestled in between, seeking warmth. He tucked his nose underneath my trouser legs. Luckily for him I was still in my two-day-old scrubs, so he was able to hide from the oncoming rain. I hauled my only bag back against the wall, attempting to keep it as dry as possible.

I had read about ferries into idyllic towns in romance novels. I had always pictured sitting out in the sun, drinking rosé, staring at the horizon and dreaming of wherever I was travelling to. Instead, my legs were going numb in two-day-old underwear and I cringed in pain as my bruised back pressed against the wall. We were departing from the south-east of England. I could do this—this was the final leg of my journey. Once I was across the water I would be safe.

The ferry started to fill up. It could only take a few cars. Surely they weren't going to drag this out any further to wait for the one driver who fancied visiting this remote island—it was hardly a tourist destination.

Sospes was a small island off the south-east coast of England. Unlike on other islands, the residents did all they could to avoid the remote landscape becoming a holiday spot. There were no all-inclusive hotels, no cheesy gift shops and no other ways to get onto the island. Even the ferry deterred potential holidaymakers, since it only travelled to Sospes twice a week.

Half the small population of Sospes was made up of people who'd been born on the island like their families had been generations before. The other half had moved their lives to the island, looking for the translation of the name—'safety'.

I could see the outline of a larger vehicle approaching, a bright cherry red. My eyes felt as if they were blurring, or maybe it was the increasing rain. Giving up, exhausted from the past few days, I closed my eyes and held my dachshund tight with one arm looped around my bag. I started to drift off to sleep, encouraged by the monotonous rhythm of the waves.

Ben

We boarded the small ferry to go back home. I'd always had my doubts that it could take the fire engine, but Gavin the ferryman insisted he could take four fire engines. Ours was the only one on the island, so I never knew how well this had been tested.

Jim always drove and I sat up front. I preferred to stay out of the conversations that were happening between the four men behind me. I could only take so much of Mike talking about his late-night encounters.

We parked up to the right of the wheelhouse, where Gavin took his place, ready to take us back home. The rain was hammering down to the point of drowning out Mike just as he got to, "And then when she took off her pants, you couldn't imagine what she had down there …"—something I'd try not to imagine.

I used my sleeve to wipe the inside of the window to my left. Glancing down at the shelter, I had to double-take. "Jim, am I going mad or is someone sat down there?"

Jim leant towards my window and nodded. "Aye, a girl … and what's that in her lap, is that a rat?"

Without thinking, I opened the door and stepped down out of the engine into the heavy rain.

"Oi, keep that door shut. My balls are shrinking back here," Trent cried from directly behind me.

"Shut up, Trent," replied a chorus from Jim and a couple of the guys in the back, who had noticed where I was heading.

As I crossed the small distance between us, my heartbeat rapidly increased and my body started to go into work mode. I was no stranger to a damsel in distress—I'd walked into many situations where I didn't know the outcome—but adrenaline coursed through my body. Something didn't seem right.

Rosie

Strong hands grabbed hold of my shoulders and shook lightly. Flinching, I used all the strength I could muster to push my legs back to create distance between myself and the unknown hands. Doug, my dachshund, sprang to life, growling at the stranger in front of me. My eyes frantically darted around, my breathing speeding up.

"Hey, it's okay. Sorry, I shouldn't have grabbed you. Are you okay?" the stranger asked, his face tilting to the side as he looked at me. His eyes were a deep brown, his face mostly covered by a dark beard. A scar ran down the left side of his face, a lighter pigment compared to his tanned skin. His scrutinising gaze softened as his eyes lifted back to mine.

"I'm okay," I answered pathetically, only managing to echo his words, increasingly aware of the pain I could feel in my ribs as I pressed further into the wheelhouse.

"You don't look it. Come sit in the engine for the crossing. You shouldn't be sat out here in the rain, sweetheart."

He hadn't actually asked me anything. He had told me. Indignant and channelling my incandescent need to be independent, I stared into his dark eyes. "No."

"No? I don't think you heard me, sweetheart. I said come sit in the engine. Now."

Before I had the chance to argue, he had picked up my bag, hiked Doug up under his arm and returned to the bright red engine. I stared at his back as he retreated with everything I owned under his arms. I didn't have much choice but to follow him. Begrudgingly, I tried to stand up, grabbing at my right side in sudden pain as I leant too much weight on it.

He returned and looked at me with a face full of worry, his dark brows pinched together, his lips forming a straight line. He got back down to my level; his hands hovered by my sides as I got to my feet. Trying to hide the wincing, I turned back towards the engine, where I could see Doug sat looking out of the window on the lap of someone else. Sure, dachshunds were meant to be loyal until it was time to decide between being warm and dry or wet and cold.

The stranger's arm wrapped around my waist and guided me by his side as he silently supported my attempt to get back towards the engine. He spoke through his clenched teeth. "I can see you're in pain. We're all firefighters. We can help, we're medically trained."

I stopped and turned to him, trying to stop my eyes from rolling out of my head. "And do you think I'm in fancy dress?" I motioned down to my hospital scrubs, evidence of my medical training.

He glared down at me, eyes narrowing as they took in my whole body, from my wild, unruly hair, now wet and plastered against my head, giving the illusion of a drowned lion, down to my sodden Converse squelching as I took each step. I shouldn't have drawn attention to myself. I guessed I didn't look too capable in that moment.

Ben

Messy hair framed her round face. She had bright green eyes and a cautious, watchful stare. She didn't want to be rescued by me. I didn't care—I wasn't going to leave her and her pathetic excuse for a dog sat outside in the freezing rain whilst we had plenty of room.

Opening the front door to the cab, I gestured for her to stand in front of me. She took a sharp inhale of breath as she raised one of her short legs to reach the steps. Stepping forward, I effortlessly lifted her up so she was between myself and Jim. She looked back at me, visibly frustrated with my need to help. *If only she knew how much I instantly want to look after her.* Shaking off that thought, I ignored her and sat down, shutting us in from the persistent rain.

She turned to look behind us, where she saw her dog nestled into Mike's lap. Mike was taking selfies of himself and the small dog, clearly trying to gain more female Instagram followers. She turned back round. Our eyes locked and she gave me a small smirk.

Okay, progress.

The silence was deafening inside the engine. This wasn't my usual loud, boisterous team. I turned round to the rest of my crew and pointed at our new hitchhiker beside me, feeling embarrassed I didn't even know her name. "Lads, this is …" I looked at her questioningly.

"Rosie," she responded, locking eyes again, then quickly looking away. She wouldn't give me the eye contact I was craving. "Thank you for the ride. Once we get to the other side, I'll be fine to walk."

Disregarding her last comment, I continued. "Lads, this is Rosie, we're giving her a lift to her final destination. Behave now, we're not used to having a lady on board."

Again, those dazzling green eyes were rolling back. Clearly she wasn't impressed with us treating her any differently. Ignoring her reaction, I leant back behind me, reaching for a towel. She smiled as she took the towel from me, wincing again in pain.

"You all right, love?" Jim asked, noticing the sharp intake of breath.

"Yes, fine. Please, I'm fine. Just ignore me. I'm fine."

Jim and I shared a worried look.

The journey across the sea continued and the steady waves rocked Rosie to sleep. Her head rested against my shoulder, then slipped down onto my lap. Without thinking I lifted my hand to stroke her chestnut-brown hair, which was now starting to curl as it dried. I brushed it out of her face, which showed signs of bruising under her eyes, and I could feel a cut disappearing under her hairline. What had happened to her? A surge of heat rose to my head as I filled with anger. Who or what would hurt her? She looked so harmless, so young. She had to be only in her early twenties. I would have said younger if I hadn't removed her lanyard from around her neck. She was an emergency department nurse, so had to be at least twenty-one.

Trent leant forward and muttered in my ear, "She's covered in bruises, mate, do you think we should take her to the police station?" Trent's brows furrowed as he looked down at Rosie peacefully sleeping in my lap.

"I mean, why was she a walking passenger on a ferry, did you hear her accent? She's way too posh to be from round here. This doesn't feel right. She's got one bag, a dog … I reckon she's running."

I matched his concern. She didn't share our southern English twang. "Let's just let her sleep for now. She's safe here with us. She doesn't need to run." My hand returned to the soothing stroke across her hair.

She was small, petite, with soft curves. She must have been about five feet, with long dark curly hair and rosy lips. She looked so tranquil sleeping in my lap, as if this were where she belonged. I noticed more bruising across her cheekbone and on the bridge of her nose. My heart started to ache when I thought about what had happened to Rosie.

"Thank God for that! We're finally here. I don't think I could have done much more of that swaying," Jim cheered, excitedly starting the engine, preparing to take the truck off of the ferry and onto land. "Where are we dropping Sleeping Beauty off then? No point starting the journey if she's heading to the east side of the island."

Feeling upset knowing I had to wake her, I whispered in her ear. "Rosie, sweetheart, we need to know where to take you."

She looked up at me with sleepy eyes, stretching underneath me, then suddenly jolted up as if she had just remembered where she was. She let out a small cry and grabbed at her stomach as she sat up. Everyone went silent, looking at her.

"Erm, I'm going to my brother's, he lives on Cherry Lane, do you know it? I don't have signal. I don't even have battery. My phone died yesterday, useless thing." She tried to fill the silence, attempting to distract us from the sound she had just made.

Reaching out, I brushed the back of my hand against the side of her soft face. "Rosie, what happened to you?"

Her eyes started to brim with tears and without warning she swatted my hand away. "Please don't touch me." She turned to Jim. "Can you take me there?"

"Yes, of course, love," he replied in a soothing and very unlike Jim tone.

With her frown disappearing, Rosie sat back in her seat, staring forward at the road ahead.

Rosie

The rest of the journey was uneventful. I managed to avoid any more moments with the nameless man sat next to me, but his eyes continued to bore into the side of my head. The silence was deafening. I couldn't stand there being a space for anyone to think too much about me or share any more of the worried looks that I had seen passed around the engine.

With an abrupt burst of confidence and determination, I turned my body to face him as gently as I could. "What's your name?" His eyes flicked up to mine, refocusing his attention from whatever daydream he was caught in. "I need to know in case you try to murder me or something," I added, trying to play it cool.

"Oh, yeah, sorry. My name is Ben, Benjamin Bradley. And for the record, I'm not planning on murdering you." He chuckled as I raised the corners of my mouth slightly back.

"Nice to meet you, Ben Bradley."

"You too, Ms … Rosie?" He looked at me to answer.

"Robinson, Rosie Robinson. And it's Miss," I added with a slight blush. *Why am I blushing? Get a grip.*

"Aha! I knew I had seen your picture before. You're Archie Robinson's sister, aren't you?" Trent's voice silenced the chatter from the back.

Turning in my seat, holding my tender stomach, I scanned Trent's face to see if I recognised him. His skin was a dark olive tone, his eyes a muddy brown and his jaw chiselled into sharp lines. He was kind of beautiful—I'd guess Italian, with that dark hair.

"Nah, we haven't met, doll," Trent answered my unspoken question with a knowing tone. "I know Archie, he's a good friend. He's mentioned you and your ... situation." Noticing my panicked expression, he stopped talking.

Exhaling, I nodded at him, grateful he hadn't shared anything else. Ben looked between the two of us, staring past me at Trent, who was now avoiding his attempt at eye contact.

"So, why were you on the mainland if you're the fire brigade for Sospes?" I tried to pull Ben's attention, eager to change the subject.

Defeated, Ben turned back to face me, stretching his arm across the back of both our seats. "We had to go pick up some hose and decided to make it into a trip—team bonding, if you like."

I started to giggle. *Does he even realise what he just said?* As if it was infectious, laughter erupted from behind me until it filled the whole engine.

Ben looked down at me, shaking his head affectionately. "Not that kind of *hoes*. Not today, anyway," he added, winking as he gazed intensely at me.

My stomach dropped. *Oh, shit. Another man in my life is definitely not what I need.*

Focusing back on the road, I sat up eagerly as I saw the sign for Cherry Lane. "Number twelve, please." I gave Jim a thankful smile.

"Here we are, number twelve, Cherry Lane," Ben muttered beside me. *Why does he sound disappointed? I'm an idiot—it can't be about me.*

I shared a quick smile with him, then busied myself picking up things I had dropped on the journey. The engine pulled up outside the row of terraced housing. Cherry Lane was a small avenue off of one of the two main roads on the island. Twelve houses in total formed this avenue, which was lined with evergreen trees. This was considered central—if you followed along the road you'd find yourself in the town square where the few shops lined the streets.

Ben jumped out and helped me down the steps. I chose not to fight him this time, increasingly aware of the aches that consumed my whole body.

He looked down at me, cupping my face with his huge calloused hands. "Sweetheart, are you sure you don't want us to take you to hospital first to make sure you're okay?"

I shook my head in response, almost too quick, causing me to feel dizzy. Trent knocked on the navy door of number twelve. Opening the rounded door, Archie took one look at Trent and started with those man-hug greetings they did. Archie took pride in his appearance, sporting a pair of tight fitted green trousers and a cashmere jumper to match. His dark curly hair styled neatly and his facial hair perfectly trimmed.

Trent's face wasn't mirroring Archie's joy in seeing his friend. He spoke quietly, but I could see the concern from here. He was talking about me.

Archie looked up, scanning the small crowd of firefighters who had gotten out of the truck, all helping with my one bag, and the tiny dachshund still sleeping blissfully in Mike's toned arms. Archie locked eyes with me. His shoulders dropped in relief that I was safe. That I had finally left *him*.

I gave Archie what I hoped was a reassuring nod and smile. Then, all at once, my body, registering I was safe, stopped.

Ben

Rosie walked towards her brother, the corners of her mouth lifting slightly, when she abruptly dropped to the ground in front of us.

Trent, who had made his way back to the engine, dived underneath Rosie, cushioning her head from the concrete, his body scraping against the pavement. Time stood still as we paused, looking at each other, before jumping into work mode. You could feel the adrenaline coursing through the firefighters surrounding Rosie.

Jim rushed back to the engine, grabbed the oxygen, and raced to secure the clear mask on Rosie's paling face. Mike was already starting his initial assessment; Mike had completed four years of medical school before he'd decided to retrain as a firefighter, so we usually let him lead any medical situation. He looked past me to the guys circling us in the bitter rain. "Get the medic bag!"

Why didn't I take her to the hospital? I knew I shouldn't have listened to her. Fuck, Rosie.

The colour had now completely drained from her face. She was starting to look slightly grey. Mike shoved scissors in my hand, motioning for me to cut open Rosie's clothes whilst he fiddled with the defibrillator in preparation as Jim took over checking her pulse. This didn't feel right— although I had only just met this girl, I knew she'd hate us all looking at her. *I* hated everyone looking at her.

Steadying my hands, I unzipped Rosie's hoodie and carefully cut down the middle of her scrubs, ready to expose the injuries she had been guarding. I fixated on the logo of the hospital she worked at. *Shit, that's miles away.*

An eerie silence fell upon us. A few sharp inhales of breath and a "Fucking hell" from behind me drew my eyes back to focus fully on her partly exposed body.

"Ben, she's covered in them, everywhere." Mike beckoned for me to look as he lifted up her sleeves and slightly lowered her scrub trousers to expose her pale skin.

Rosie was covered in bruises, linear red marks and healing cuts across her whole body.

Standing up, I had to get away from what I could see in front of me. My blood pounded around my body, awoken by the fury that was building inside me. Clenching my fists, I moved out of the way and turned to face her brother, who had his hands glued to his face as he watched on in pure horror.

"I'm going to have to call the police." I focused on the beads of sweat forming across his brow, daring him to challenge my decision.

Archie looked towards me blankly, then realised what I had said. "Yeah. Of course … yeah, I don't have any problem with the police knowing. She will, though." His matching green eyes flicked back to Rosie as he shook his head.

Does he know something? Anger started to build in me again. *Did he know his sister was in danger and he allowed this to happen?*

"She's back!" Mike shouted back across the scene, his hand on her shoulder as she started to stir. "Rosie, angel, stay still. You're in good hands. You're going to be fine."

My legs almost gave way as I walked back towards them. Kneeling down beside her, I whispered tenderly against her ear, "You're safe now, sweetheart."

CHAPTER 2

The One with All the Beeps

Rosie

Beep. Beep. Beep.

The continuous tones of the machines around me filled my mind. *Where am I? Were the handsome firefighters all a dream? Am I back at work?*

"Nooo!" My body jolted and I screamed across the dark room. I couldn't have dreamt it all. *He* would be here to pick me up from work soon, and I couldn't go back. I couldn't do this any longer.

Dark eyes startled me, and a strong hand guided me to lie back down. "Rosie, you're having a nightmare. You're in hospital, but it's okay. You're safe."

"But he knows where I am, I have to leave!" The words came out before I could orientate myself. I reached out in front of me, finding strong, corded arms, trailing down till my hand covered his. I stretched my fingers to feel for *his* rings, which usually adorned each finger—they weren't there. Steadying myself, I took a huge inhale, taking with me an unfamiliar smell of smoke. I sucked in another breath, searching for that usual warning smell of whisky upon his breath—it didn't come.

The hand where mine rested came into focus. Dark tattoos covered his bronzed skin, a dusting of dark hair. A green and white hospital gown covered my small body. The stripes were worlds away from the royal blue scrubs I wore at work.

He wasn't here. My mind drifted back to the last couple of days. This was real, I had escaped. Relief flooded my mind as I looked back at the man in front of me. I nodded once and drifted back to sleep.

Beep. Beep. Beep.

Light was shining through the stained vertical blinds, casting a shadow across the room. Reflections danced across my body. I was dressed in mint-green stripes. Glancing at an IV stuck in my hand and the fluid bag hooked above my head, I searched for any clues that might tell me what was wrong with me. I shifted uncomfortably where I was sat. *Oh, for fuck's sake, they've catheterised me.* Feeling the urge to wee, knowing I could but didn't want to with a catheter in, was a torturous and inhumane feeling. My brain was having a standoff with my bladder.

My focus was momentarily distracted by an old episode of *Friends* on the small TV set. Then I noticed a large hand that didn't belong to me holding on to the bed rails to my right. When I tracked the hand up to the body, it was connected to … Benjamin fucking Bradley. And he was asleep. *What is he doing here?*

Not wanting to have an awkward conversation when he woke up, I closed my eyes and allowed my head to relax against the pillow, hoping he'd be gone when I next opened my eyes.

Beep. Beep. Beep.

An extreme thirst awoke me from my medicated sleep and caused me to bolt up in my bed. I needed a tap, a puddle, anything I could quench my thirst with. A jug of water on the table at the end of the bed taunted me. I looked around for my call bell. *Oh, that's great—hooked above my head, just out of reach.*

Ben was sleeping in an armchair beside me, his huge frame curled up. *What the fuck? How is he still asleep? Wake up and get me water!*

My voice had gone. I only managed a feeble whisper, my mouth was so dry. I looked around for something to throw at him to get his attention. *Bingo! A thermometer.* Without thinking, I picked it up and threw it at Ben's head. Growing up playing cricket in the street with my brothers had given me an excellent aim.

Ben

Something hard knocked the side of my head, waking me abruptly. My eyes darted back to the girl sat in the bed beside me, who was now chuckling to herself. I softened as soon as I saw her grinning at me. "Rosie."

She frowned as she tried to act out something to me, lifting her hand and tilting it by her mouth.

I stared blankly at her for a moment before clicking. "Hold on, let me go check with a nurse."

She nodded, giving me a sarcastic thumbs-up.

I left, then rushed back into the room, holding a pissed-off nurse by the arm. "Rosie's awake and she wants a drink." I looked expectantly at the nurse, getting annoyed as she just stared back at me.

"Is that what the big drama was, hon?" She tutted as she turned away from me. It wasn't a drama, but if she delayed giving Rosie what she wanted, it certainly would be. "Rose, dear, thirsty, are you? That's not a problem. Small sips, dear," she coaxed Rosie, helping her lift her cup to take a drink.

Rosie looked up at her gratefully. A rare feeling of jealousy came over me. I desperately wanted to be the one to look after her.

Once Rosie had finished her drink, the nurse propped her up on her pillow, repositioning her. Rosie squeaked out a request to the nurse, barely audible. The nurse nodded, then proceeded to usher me out of the room.

"I'm not going."

"For this, hon, you'll have to. You can come back right in after we've made Rose a bit more comfortable."

Scowling at the nurse for calling her Rose, I retreated back into the corridor and headed towards the family room.

Entering the low-lit room, I was met by anxious faces. Archie was with his husband Simon, who had joined him, both wearing matching frowns. Simon had a protective arm around his husband, anchoring him in place. Archie looked like he wanted to be anywhere but here, his eyes darting towards the door as if it was his chance for escape. Most of my fire crew were still there as well, including Mike, Trent and Jim, who stood up as I entered the room.

"She's awake," I announced, relief flooding over me as I sat down beside Jim. "She'll probably want to see you, Archie." I looked over at him—he looked a mess. I thought the guilt had finally caught up with him. He didn't reply.

Simon cleared his throat. "Thank you, Ben, thank you, everyone, but I think I'll get my husband home to rest. She seems like she's safe." He looked knowingly over at me.

"You should all go home too; I can stay with her," I said. "I've phoned Rich down at the police station to come and see her. Suppose I better be here."

Jim stood up, clasping my shoulder. "Let Rosie know we were here; I know we've only just met, but she's a sweet girl. We'll pop by tomorrow with some supplies." The rest of my team stood up and exited behind Jim.

Mike hung back, staring uncomfortably down at his feet. "Boss, I know you're feeling attached to her, but go easy, she must have been through a lot. She needs to feel secure right now. Don't make your usual mistakes." Taken aback by Mike's comments, I stared back at him, my eyes narrowing. "What would Dina say about you playing protector to Rosie? You know she's still bitter and you have to see her every shift at the station. Don't make another girl any promises you don't plan on keeping."

"Go home, Mike," was all I could manage. He nodded at me, then walked down the silent corridor to catch up with Trent.

It was a low blow to bring up Dina. He and Dina both knew that it was just casual, and for him to make it sound like anything more was laughable. It wasn't my fault she wanted more. Yeah, it was awkward seeing her every shift changeover, but that was hardly my fault.

Disregarding Mike's warning, I headed back to see Rosie. Pausing outside the door of her room, I looked in, expecting to see her resting in her bed. It was empty. "Rosie?"

A crash came from inside the bathroom. I marched across the room and tore open the door without any hesitation. Rosie was sat on the toilet, hospital gown bunched up above her waist, commode upended on the floor beside her. She stared at me with wide eyes before shouting as loud as she could manage. "Get the fuck out!"

I didn't plan on moving. "You shouldn't be doing things alone, where's that fucking nurse gone?"

"I'm. Fine. Get. Out," Rosie shouted between deep inhales of breath. I turned round to face the door, but didn't move, squeezing my eyes together to distract myself from the bruises I saw all over her legs.

Rosie, now realising I wasn't going to leave her alone, flushed the toilet and let out a sigh to signal she was done. I lifted her up off the toilet and steadied her at the sink by wrapping my arms gently round her tiny waist.

After she had washed her hands for what felt like a lifetime, I scooped her up, holding her close to my chest, and walked back into the room. She looked like she wanted to fight me about the way I was holding her, but she also looked too exhausted to argue. Picking her battles, she allowed me to lay her back against her pillows and tuck her into her hospital sheets and blue knitted blanket.

She looked up at me, her face scrunched up in confusion. "Why are you here?" she blurted out.

"I don't know, but I know I can't leave you." Reaching up, I pushed a stray hair behind her ear. She leant into my touch. "What happened to you, Rosie?"

"Nothing, please don't ask me, I'm fine. I'm here, I'm fine now." She jerked away.

"That would mean a lot more if we hadn't had to almost use a defibrillator on you a few hours ago. Fucking look around, Rosie, you're not fine. I've spoken to a friend, Rich, who works at the local police station. He'll be here soon." I went to sit back down on the chair next to Rosie when she let out a cry.

"No! You can't. I won't speak to the police. No! How dare you. He will *kill* me. You don't know what you've done!" The genuine fear painted all over her face only fuelled my rage.

"Rosie, just calm down, please don't get upset. You need to be calm, you're safe here. You've got me now; I'm not going to let anyone do anything to you." My large hand engulfed her small hands, pushing them down beside her as she tried to lash out, attempting to get out of the bed.

"Oh, yeah, you're going to stay with me all the time, are you?" she sneered at me, fire in those green eyes. "How do you know anything about what he'll do? You know nothing. Leave me the fuck alone. I don't even know why you're still here; I don't know you!" She was lashing out, and me being in front of her was only aggravating her further. Stepping away, I was distracted momentarily by the rising beeps of her monitoring machine. Her heart rate was climbing higher. The alarm sounded.

A nurse appeared in the doorway. "I think you'd better leave. Let her settle down and have some sleep."

Rosie squealed, trying again to push herself out of bed, fighting against the pain she was suffering.

"Rosie, dear, you really shouldn't be moving. You have four broken ribs and lots of very sore bruising, darling," the nurse soothed, trying to keep Rosie calm with her matronly manner. Rosie wasn't calming down—she was getting increasingly angry, thrashing about her bed, trying to disconnect her tubes.

The nurse hit the call button above the bed. A team of doctors and nurses swiftly entered, pushing me back further against the magnolia walls.

"Get the sedation!" the nurse barked above the sounds of Rosie kicking out and screaming in the faces of the blasé junior doctors. I watched from opposite the end of her bed, helpless. Frozen.

A nurse stealthily approached Rosie, grabbed her thigh, and stabbed a needle into her already bruised skin. It took all of my strength to stop myself from running towards her. Rosie started to relax, her shouts became more slurred and slowed until the team were able to position her back in bed and reconnect her IV and monitoring. They all left, unfazed by what they had just seen.

The nurse who'd first entered gave my shoulder a small, sympathetic pat. "She should be okay for a while now, hon."

My mouth opened and shut as I looked back at her. *What the fuck have I just witnessed?* It was my fault—as soon as I'd told Rosie I had called the police she'd flipped out and wanted to leave. She'd been so scared, and I'd known then that I needed to protect her.

Unable to sleep that night, I stared fixedly at her in the bed, the bruising on her arms now more visible in her baggy hospital gown. If I ever found out who'd done this to her, I would kill them.

I saw every hour pass. I didn't need to look at the clock—I was awake every time a nurse came in to check in on Rosie, giving me a reassuring nod or smile after they had done her observations.

Rosie's face was lit up by the numerous machines surrounding the bed, her lips slightly parted as she slept, her eyes shut. She looked peaceful whilst she was sleeping. I couldn't help but think it was due to the sedation. It didn't matter—I was grateful to whatever made her feel at peace. Staring at her in her serene state allowed me to also feel calm and finally drift off to sleep.

Rosie

Beep. Beep. Beep.

Oh, balls, not this again. I gingerly opened one eyelid to see if my visitor had left me alone yet. I huffed and squeezed my eyes shut when I saw that he was still sat in that stupid chair, refusing to leave me. I let out a loud, exaggerated sigh.

Stop being a bitch, Rosie, why are you trying to wake him up? Looking around the room, I understood what must have happened. *The fuckers sedated me.* No wonder I'd woken up so grouchy. Embarrassed about what he must have witnessed, I covered my face with my hands and let out an involuntary moan.

"Are you okay, sweetheart?" A hesitant voice came from beside me.

"I'm fine. Please can we not speak about last night? I'm feeling really embarrassed."

Ben looked over at me, pursed his lips and nodded. I could tell he wasn't happy not talking about it, but he let it go, at least for now.

"Ben, I'm really not trying to be rude, but why are you still here?"

He looked almost deflated. "Well, who else is here?" he bit back.

Looking back around the depressingly dim room, I realised he was right. I was alone.

Noticing the effect of his words on me, he stood up and sat down at the end of my bed. "Rosie, I'm sorry, that was mean. Your brother and his husband were here—I told them to leave." He scrubbed his hand over his dark beard. "Couldn't leave you."

He was still there after everything that had happened the night before. I wasn't used to someone hanging around—people usually gave up on me. There was something comforting about having him by my side. He made me feel protected, and that was all I'd ever wanted.

Ben

A small smile tipped up the edges of her rosy lips. We kept eye contact, staring intently at each other until she pinched her eyebrows together and asked, "My brother got married?"

I smiled back at her. She looked so adorable in her shapeless hospital gown. "I guess so. Trent knows your brother. I've only just met him. Simon seems all right." I didn't want to talk about her brother, I wanted to talk about her. "I need to go make a few phone calls and sort some things out. Do you think you'll be okay by yourself?"

Her face fell. I hadn't been expecting that. She had been so adamant about not needing me yesterday, she hadn't shown any sign she wanted me there.

"Actually, Jim will be able to sort out everything at the station. Time I gave him more responsibility."

Her smile returned as she peeled back part of her blanket, wincing as she shuffled over to the right of the bed so her side was right against the bed rail. I looked at her, confused and irritated that she was causing herself harm. She needed to rest. Why was she such a bad patient?

She patted the bed where she had just created space. "Please sit next to me, I think I need a cuddle."

My heart swelled at her small request. I could tell she was uncomfortable asking from the desperation in her voice. *She may not want me here, but she does need me.* Standing up slowly, I kicked off my work boots as I took my phone, wallet and lighter out of my pocket and eased myself onto the bed, making sure I wouldn't knock her. Her eyes sparkled with unshed tears. I placed my arm back around the top of the bed, creating space for her to rest her head against me.

She let out a deep exhale. I didn't want to touch her, she was so fragile and was bruised everywhere. I didn't know what to do with my spare arm. I fiddled with the blanket, which I had pulled back over us. Rosie reached out and held my hand in hers, nestled her head against my chest and closed her eyes. "Thank you, Ben."

Planting a soft kiss on the top of her head, I closed my eyes too.

Our breaths became in sync, both steadying, as together we fell asleep.

Rosie

Beep. Beep. Beep.

Uncurling my legs, I stretched them out in front of me. Ben was still asleep, and I didn't want to wake him. I couldn't tell what time it was and didn't know where my phone had gone. Or my dog.

A gentle knock on the door distracted me from the whereabouts of my dachshund. Jim, Mike and Trent stood sheepishly looking at their fire captain curled up in my hospital bed. Raising my hand in an awkward wave, I smiled shyly at the three of them, then beckoned them to enter the room.

"Hi," I whispered. They all stood grinning down at me in their uniforms. Bloody hell, I'd forgotten how good-looking they all were.

I stared down at the man in my bed. Bloody hell, he was also really good-looking. He was slightly taller and broader than the other men at the door, who were leaner. He had dark unruly hair and a dark beard, or had he just not shaved? Either way, he looked hot.

"Sorry to bother you, Rosie, love, we just wanted to check to see how you were." Jim's voice had a slight Australian twang. Jim was blond with short messy hair and bright blue eyes. He looked slightly older than the other two.

I looked back at his reassuring gaze and let out what I thought was an encouraging smile, suddenly wincing in pain. "I'm fine, thank you, Jim. And thank you for everything, but where's my dog?"

The three men laughed together.

"He's with your brother, doll, he's fine, don't worry." Trent looked over at Ben, still asleep in the bed.

Jim stepped forward, placing a carrier bag on the end of my bed. "We thought you might want some of your things."

Reaching into the bag, I pulled out my toothbrush and a soft knitted jumper, and at the bottom of the bag was my favourite book. My eyes widened. "You brought me my book?" He shrugged one of his shoulders. I held the worn copy of *Alice in Wonderland* close to my chest. "Thank you," was all I could manage; he had no idea how much comfort the folded pages and cracked spine brought me.

"Uh, we've also come to check in on Ben. He didn't show up to work today and we were worried. We can wake him if you want. You don't look very comfortable, and you need to be careful with your injuries."

"No. Don't wake him. I'm fine. Honestly, I'm fine." I looked back at the men, now clearly struggling with what to do next. I was sure they could sense the comfort he was giving me.

"Rosie, I know you don't know us, but we're going to be here for you. You've got a whole team of us now who will have your back. You'll be safe here on the island. If you ever need anything, you can come to us, doll."

Trent's comments stunned me momentarily. I hadn't realised how much I needed to hear that. Letting out an involuntary sniffle, I raised my book in front of my mouth to stifle the rest of the sobs my body was so desperate to release.

Panicking, Mike rushed round to me and tried to put his comforting arm around me, navigating Ben's broad shoulders. Waking to the sounds of my sobs, Ben opened his eyes and stared at me, then at Mike, then back to me where I was trying but failing to hide my tears. He sat up straight and glared at Mike. "What the fuck did you do?"

"He did nothing. He did nothing. It was me. I'm sorry," I managed between sobs. Ben motioned for the boys to leave, then pulled me closer for a hug, holding me silently and allowing me to cry into his safe arms.

CHAPTER 3

Recovery-ish

Ben

Rosie was going home. The nurses had sorted out all her discharge paperwork, medication, and dressings by ten o'clock that morning. Rosie's brother still hadn't visited. I couldn't help but feel this was because of the guilt he was feeling. *Selfish prick.*

Rosie looked up at me, clearly thinking the same thing. "Um, where am I going once I leave here? Does my brother still want me there? He hasn't been in to see me," she added in a small voice that instantly made me want to punch her brother in the face.

Kneeling down by her bed, I helped to put her Converse trainers back on. "Of course they want you there." My heart felt heavy at the idea of leaving her. I hoped her brother would know what to do if she woke up panicked again or needed a cuddle or needed to cry.

"Okay, good. He's a good brother, he just doesn't do hospitals. We spent a lot of time in hospital waiting rooms when we were younger. My mum wasn't very well …" She trailed off, stopping herself before disclosing anything further.

"I've put my number in your phone. It's so you can contact me if you ever need anything, anything at all, Rosie." I smiled down at her puzzled expression. "Please text me, Rosie, I've become quite attached to you."

She let out a cute giggle and looked up at me. "I've become quite attached to you too."

Rosie was still weak and wobbly on her feet, so I steadied her by holding her close to my side. She was still in a lot of pain, so the walk back through the hospital was slow, but I didn't mind, as it was more time spent with Rosie before I had to say goodbye. We walked towards my awaiting pickup truck. Rosie stared around the car park. "Where's the fire engine?"

I laughed at her genuine question. "Rosie, the fire engine's not my car. This is us." I pointed towards the black truck. Still holding on to Rosie's arm, I opened the passenger door, putting my hands around her waist as I lifted her in. Fastening her seat belt, carefully avoiding her ribs, I stretched over and plugged in the belt. As I leaned across her, our eyes met. Rosie stretched her hand out and stroked my face, reaching down across my beard.

"I can't do this," she said, dropping her hands to her lap, where they knotted together nervously.

"Do what?" I knew what she was saying, but I needed to hear it from her.

"I can't be with you; I can't be with anyone. If you knew what I've been through you'd understand. I'm sorry … I wish I were normal." Tears started to fill her eyes again. She couldn't look me in the eyes and had lost the spark I had seen during short moments in the hospital. She was scared.

"It's okay. I understand." Sure, I understood trauma and wanting to detach yourself from everyone around you. It didn't help lessen the sting. "I will still be here for you, Rosie, and I don't think I'll be able to leave you alone."

She still didn't look at me. I checked her seat belt again. Shutting her door, I walked round the back of the truck, ensuring she couldn't see me. I buried my face in my hands, rubbing my palms against my forehead. What was wrong with me? Why did she have this effect on me? I knew I wouldn't be able to stay away. She was mine, even though she didn't know it yet. She was mine and I needed to protect her. I hated what she had been through.

I dropped Rosie at her brother's house, where Archie and Simon met her. Simon shook my hand as Archie ushered his sister inside, closing the door behind them.

"This is my number." I wrote it down. "Please, if you need anything or if she freaks out or needs a friend or anything, call me."

Simon nodded and smiled knowingly. I didn't get to say goodbye to Rosie, but it was best that way. I never wanted to say goodbye to her.

CHAPTER 4

Rosé-Tinted Glasses

Rosie

It had been five weeks. Five weeks that I hadn't left the house. Five weeks that I hadn't seen or heard from Ben.

The physical pain had been replaced with a dark cloud of emotional torture. These past five weeks had been hell. I'd had nightmare after nightmare, daily panic attacks and constant anxiety, but I wouldn't let them call Ben. He had done enough—he needed someone normal, not a tainted mess like me. He hadn't reached out either. He'd probably forgotten about me. Could hardly blame him. I was forgettable.

Archie and Simon had been the rays of sunshine shining through the dark cloud that followed me. Archie would sit with me most days, both drinking rosé until he got too drunk or stressed and couldn't deal with my anxiety, then calm Simon would take over. They loved having Doug— they walked him each day. It was their time together where they didn't have to look after me or think about me.

Finally, I had grown some ovaries and was ready to leave the safe confines of number twelve. I was feeling claustrophobic inside their beautiful home. Flicking through a newspaper, I noticed an advert for a local fair. The fair was in the town, raising money for the school roof. It didn't take much to convince Archie and Simon to let us go. I was getting bored and needed something other than rosé to busy my mind and numb my thoughts.

Rummaging through the minimal clothes I had packed with me, I found a powder-blue wrap dress that tucked in at the waist. The scars had mostly faded, so this was a safe bet. I paired the dress with my Converse and a knitted cardigan and decided to blow-dry my hair and style it straight. I used the little bits of makeup I had to add some concealer to hide my under-eye bags, give off the illusion that I had my shit together.

Simon's mouth dropped when he saw me. "Bloody hell, Rosie, if you floated my boat, I'd be all over you. You look amazing. It's good to see you looking so … so … human." He smiled apologetically, looking down at my legs. "Oh, and you even shaved your legs!"

Throwing my head back, I laughed at his comment. *Oh, wow, this feels good.*

The street was lit up by festoon lights overlapping the bunting. I hadn't realised how pretty this lane was when we'd first arrived. My mind had clearly been elsewhere.

It had only taken us ten minutes along the footpath to get into the main village. There was a gazebo set up in the town square where a band were playing, the sound of a folky guitar echoing across the space. Lining the square, lots of makeshift tents were selling their wares. It was a sensory overload; I squinted my eyes at the brightness of all the coloured tents around me and my stomach growled at the smell of popcorn. The bright signs, laughter and lights were a lot more than I was used to from staying inside the house for five weeks.

We made our way through the busy streets, only stopping when Archie and Simon introduced me to someone they knew. They told everyone we met that I was visiting. I had no intention of going home.

"Oi, stranger!"

I couldn't help but smile when I saw Jim jogging towards us. The good-looking blond man grinned back at me, but his smile tipped down as he got closer. It wasn't hard to understand why. I had barely eaten and my clothes didn't fit me as well as they used to, hanging lifelessly on my emaciated body. My eyes still had dark circles underneath despite my best effort at concealing them. I could tell he could see the sadness I was desperately trying to mask.

Snapping myself out of my mood, I gave him what I thought was a reassuring smile. It felt weird to have a reason to smile again. He was wearing a uniform, the grey shirt tight across his broad shoulders. Did that mean that the rest of the team was there? Who was I kidding—I didn't care about the team, I just wanted to see Ben.

"It's really good to see you, love, we've been thinking about you. Well, we've actually been worried about you. I thought maybe we'd see you around, being a small island and all ..." His voice trailed off as he looked behind me.

Turning, I saw him. Ben was staring intently at me. He looked sad, deflated maybe. Suddenly filled with guilt that I hadn't spoken to him sooner, I raised my hand in an attempt at a casual wave. *I look like an idiot. Who even waves any more?*

His eyes didn't leave mine as he walked towards me. I could see his eyes darting down over my body, his face mirroring Jim's concerned expression. I felt really fucking self-conscious as I pulled my dress over my body, trying to make it look more fitted and less baggy over my smaller frame. I was still looking down at myself when I felt him approach me. I looked up into his dark eyes. He stood right in front of me. *What is he thinking?* He looked tired too. He reached down to me and wrapped his arms around me, pulling me into a soft, comforting hug.

My body tensed at his touch, but I allowed him to hold me. It felt like he needed it too.

An awkward cough came from behind us, interrupting our moment. I turned to see that Mike and Trent had also joined us. "Do I get one of those too, Ro-Ro?" Trent gave me a crooked grin.

I stepped over to the two men and gave them my attempt at a hug. Ben made a noise that sounded suspiciously like a growl behind us. Recognising how uncomfortable I was and how Ben had reacted, they didn't make it last as long as my embrace with Ben. *This is so awkward.*

"Well, angel, we're pleased to see you." Mike gave a sympathetic tilt of his head. He was definitely the most serious out of the four. "We've all been worrying about you. You'll stop by our booth later?"

The feeling of remorse bubbled up again. I hadn't made any contact with the men who had saved me. "I'll be sure to do that." *Probably won't do that.*

Seemingly satisfied with my answer, they turned to leave. I let out a deep exhale and my shoulders dropped with the release of the tension I'd been holding there. Turning around, I walked into a wall of muscle.

Ben looked down at me and I could tell there was more he wanted to say. It felt strange. Someone I had been so vulnerable with, sharing a bed within the hospital, stood in front of me. I really didn't know him.

Think! I need to say something to end the awkward silence and to ease this tension. "So, what's your booth selling then?" I almost sounded convincing.

"We don't need to talk about that. I haven't stopped thinking about you. Can I come by later?"

Taken off guard by his candour, I took a step back. "I'm not your problem any more, Ben. I appreciate you staying with me while I was in the hospital, but you don't need to worry about me any more. I'll be fine."

Trying to ignore the hurt etched across his face, I turned on my heel and strolled back towards my brother's house.

When I looked back over my shoulder, my stomach sank at seeing him still standing there in the same place I had disappointed him, his hands running through his messy dark hair. My chest tightened as I walked away, the guilt sitting heavy in my stomach. For the past five weeks my heart had allowed me to imagine and dream about this moment, but as soon as I'd seen him my brain stopped me from flinging my arms around him. This wasn't a fucking fairy tale. Happily ever afters didn't exist in my world. It was unrealistic for me to dream, it wouldn't be fair to drag anyone down with me. I needed to make myself better before I allowed anyone else in.

I needed a drink. I needed a glass of rosé, or a bottle, or a bottle combined with tequila. I didn't care. My constant anxiety was taking over my life. I couldn't think without having flashbacks, I couldn't walk past a nostalgic smell without flinching. Simon had returned from work one day smelling faintly of whisky. The smell had brought me straight back to being pinned down beneath *his* body as he took everything from me. The day after that flashback, I'd noticed that all the good alcohol had been removed from the house.

When I checked my phone, it was quarter to midnight. There must be a supermarket or a petrol station or something that would sell me some wine. Pulling my hoodie over my pyjamas, I slipped on my Converse and walked down the road, one eye on my phone, navigating to the nearest shop. The supermarket was lit up with blue-tinged lights and outdated music playing through the speakers. As I walked up the aisle of the supermarket, the speakers played Britney's 'Toxic'. *I'm fucking toxic.* Picking up two bottles of cheap wine, I walked towards the only open checkout.

"Rough night, love?" the bored checkout assistant asked as she eyed my pyjamas and the bottles in front of her.

"Rough year," I muttered back, not giving her any eye contact. Paying quickly and not waiting for my change, I walked out of the entrance and unscrewed the lid of one bottle and began to drink.

The familiar red of the fire engine caught my eyes. *Fuck's sake, they do not need to see me like this. I'm wearing pyjamas with watermelons on.* I used the tote bag the bored checkout lady had given me and deposited the bottles in there, pausing first to take another large swig. Deciding to try to hide, I put my hood up and walked towards the direction of the main road.

"Oi, trouble, I see you!" A booming voice echoed across the empty car park.

Fuck, fuck, fuck. I turned slowly, preventing the bottles from jingling, giving me away. I wished I had bought something else, anything else to quiet the contact between the glass.

I hoped another awkward wave would suffice. Clearly it didn't, as Trent got to me first, pulling my hood down and ruffling my messy hair. I pulled back, scowling at him.

"Bit late to be out by yourself," Mike remarked.

"Just having a walk, couldn't sleep." *Well, it isn't a full lie.*

"Are those …?" Trent started.

"Watermelons, yep," I deadpanned, daring him to say any more. *The less said about these, the better.* He kept his mouth firmly shut, but you could tell he was bursting to say more.

"We'll give you a lift home," Jim said, motioning back to the truck. "We've just been out at a shout, we were getting some food and heading back to the station."

I listened politely before declining his offer.

"Rosie, come on." Ben's voice boomed from behind the three men standing in front of me.

"Ben, I'm fine," I warned.

Ben pushed through the men and grabbed me by the elbow, gently steering me round and back towards the engine. The wine bottles betrayed me with a loud clunking.

"What the—?" Mike reached for the bag on my shoulder and embarrassed me further by pulling out two bottles, one two thirds empty. He looked down at me and shook his head. "Drinking alone at night, Rosie?" He almost sounded as if he cared, but all I heard was judgement.

"Fuck off, you lot can't judge me, you have no idea what I'm going through! I can't close my fucking eyes without seeing him. Back off." I stunned them into silence with my outburst. My hands were flailing above my head.

"Aww, doll, you're so cute when you pout." Trent laughed at me; I realised I had punctuated my rant by stamping my foot on the ground. Jim laughed at me too, Mike looked concerned, and Ben stayed silent.

Snatching my bag back off Mike, I stormed away in the opposite direction.

"Rosie, get back here, we'll give you a lift," Jim shouted. I waved my hand behind me in a motion I hoped conveyed for them to leave me alone.

Pulling out the mostly drunk bottle, I downed the rest before discarding it in a nearby bin whilst unscrewing the next one. I stumbled along the pavement, unable to keep a straight line, but my mind was starting to cloud. *Perfect.*

The roar of the big cherry engine started up, then slowed behind me. Jim hung out of the driver's seat window. "We'll just follow you home, Rosie, so you may as well get in," he warned, his voice now sombre, his Aussie accent more prominent.

"Cool," I muttered under my breath whilst taking another swig.

Ben

She was just getting more drunk. I had to look in the opposite direction and let Jim try to coax her in—I was scared I would explode.

"The fuck is she playing at?" Mike said, concern evident in his simmering tone.

"She's a wild one, but she's drunk too much now. Shall I just go grab her?" Trent asked.

Thinking about Trent with his hands on Rosie caused me to leap out of the door of the slow-moving vehicle and storm round to face her.

"She's going to get it," one of the young trainees taunted from the engine, recognising my anger as I towered over her.

"I'm going to give you one more chance to get in or I'll throw you over my shoulder and put you in myself. Please, Rosie," I added as she swayed and came to a stop in front of me, her eyes slightly unfocused, clearly drunk off her watermelon-covered ass.

"Pfft, you don't tell me what to do, no one does. Not any more." She slammed the almost-finished wine bottle into my chest. I snatched the bottle and threw it onto the other side of the road. A smash caused the men to look out of their windows as I hoisted Rosie up over my shoulders. She protested, but she wasn't strong enough. I easily opened my passenger door and tossed her down onto the seat. *This isn't right.* I felt sick in that moment, hating myself for forcing her into the engine, but I didn't know what else to do. There was no way I was leaving her drunk and alone in the middle of the night.

"Get the fuck off me," she seethed through gritted teeth, tears of frustration pouring from her eyes as she tried to kick out at me.

"Enough, Rosie, you can't keep trying to destroy your life! You have a chance at a fresh start and you're fucking it up," Jim yelled down at Rosie, to the surprise of the rest of us.

Rosie burst into tears with her head in her hands. Sobs sounded through the engine. I turned round to the trainees and commanded they get out. Jim and I as well as Mike and Trent stayed. The two young lads got out and stood against the wall, busying themselves with their phones as we dealt with a hysterical Rosie.

"Rosie, we're only saying this because we care. But it's not safe to ever drink that much or walk around the island alone." Mike spoke, his tone calm.

"Why won't you all just leave me alone?" she replied in a defeated tone as she continued to cry.

"Because we care, doll. You're stuck with us, I'm afraid," Trent answered, shrugging one of his shoulders.

"He's right," I murmured against her ear as I pulled her body close to mine. She let me guide her into my side. I wrapped one arm around her and held her close as she sobbed. She was obviously a lot more fragile than I'd first thought.

"Sorry for shouting, love," Jim said. Rosie nodded her head. "Right, you lot, get back in. Let's go," Jim shouted at the team before we headed back through the night to drop Rosie home. The only sound breaking the silent journey was Trent softly singing 'Watermelon Sugar'.

Pulling up moments later at number twelve, we watched until she got in through her front door and saw her bedroom light switch off before we left.

CHAPTER 5
Truth Hurts

Ben

It was a quiet Thursday afternoon. We were completing our mundane tasks, waiting for our next call. Ever since we'd dropped Rosie home last night, I couldn't bear to be bored or sat still, so I returned to my office and left the boys behind playing a card game. Sitting behind the desk with my head in my hands, I remembered the last time I'd seen her.

A knock interrupted my thoughts. I wasn't used to the boys knocking. A sheepish grin peered round the door, and a pair of emerald eyes stared back at me. Rosie.

Standing up quickly, I accidentally knocked paperwork off my desk as I beckoned for her to sit down. Ignoring the paperwork now on the floor, and not taking her eyes away from mine, she sat down in front me. She looked good in her dark skinny jeans and baggy jumper. Still, she looked underweight. This bothered me more than I'd thought. Trying to distract myself from how she looked, I gave her a forced smile.

She eased her right side against the metal of the chair. She still looked to be in some sort of pain. I hated seeing her like this. I wondered what it was like to see her genuinely happy without pain. I wanted to be the one to make her genuinely happy. Raising a brow, I waited for her to make the first move.

"Look, I'm sorry about before. I was being a mega-bitch and I didn't mean it. I'm an idiot sometimes, I don't always know how to regulate what I'm feeling. I don't mean to be this person; I know you're only trying to help. I'm going to be staying here for a while, so could really use a friend. I don't know anyone else here. I'm getting fed up with being sat inside that house with the same two people. Do you fancy going out with me tonight? Get some food?"

It took me a minute to answer her rant. *Why does she think so poorly of herself? I have a feeling I know why; I have a feeling she's been made to feel bad about herself for a long time.* I regained my composure. "Miss Robinson, are you asking me out on a date?"

She rolled her eyes at my reply. "It's just food. If you don't want to go, I'm sure Trent will go with me." I was instantly filled with jealousy at her suggestion and not able to hide my emotion from my face. She looked up at me quickly, recognising her mistake. "I'm joking, I don't want to take Trent. I want to take you."

My expression eased at this retort. "Rosie, you're not taking me anywhere. I'm taking you. I'll pick you up at seven." Her eyes started to roll again. "And don't roll your eyes at me again, sweetheart." I wasn't doing well at trying to hide my tyrannical nature.

She lifted herself gently off of the chair, grimacing as she shifted her weight onto her right-hand side. I walked over to her, effortlessly lifting her to her feet. She turned and headed back towards the door, stopping momentarily and with a small smile. "See you at seven then."

I smiled to myself, realising in four hours I'd see her again. Feeling warm at the idea of us spending the evening together, I busied myself in mundane paperwork.

Rosie

Slamming the door of number twelve behind me, I closed my eyes tight and steadied my breathing. With one last deep breath out, I opened my eyes again to find myself face to face with a unnerved-looking Simon.

"Everything all right, Ro?" he asked.

"Yeah, fine. I think. I don't know, maybe."

He raised an eyebrow at me and crossed his arms across his body, somehow looking taller awaiting my answer.

"I think I'm going on a date. He said he'd pick me up at seven." I glanced down at my phone, noticing the time. *I still have a few hours to get ready or cancel.*

"I'm assuming with Ben? Well, that's good, he's a good guy. It will be good for you to get out of the house and make some friends, especially as you're going to be visiting with us for a while."

I forced a smile onto my face. I knew this wasn't permanent and I knew I couldn't live with my brother forever, but the word 'visiting' felt so temporary, so uneasy and so unsafe.

I pushed the intrusive thoughts out of my head like my work-appointed therapist had told me many times before. The one condition for my workplace turning a blind eye when I turned up to work with any bruises was the agreement that I would attend regular therapy at work. I'd reluctantly agreed as this was during work hours, so he would never find out. Her name was Lucy, and she'd quickly become a safe space for me. Instead of judging and asking why I didn't leave, she'd focused on building me up to believe that I could when I was ready.

Making a mental note to get a message to Lucy to tell her I was safe, I went over to where Simon was standing and wrapped my arms around his waist, pressing my face against his chest and giving him a tight squeeze. We stood there for what felt like forever. I tried to silently say what I had been meaning to say to him through this hug. I had never been particularly good at talking or sharing my feelings. I had been told relentlessly for the last five years to stay silent, to not talk about how I was feeling and to put myself last. I had only just met Simon, but he already felt like another brother to me.

Shit, my brother. I jumped back and looked up at Simon, who hastily wiped away his tears. "Simon, do you know if Archie has spoken to—?"

"Your brother, yes. Louis will be here later. I'm sorry, Rosie, we thought it was best they knew you were here. He's worried about you and upset. He didn't know, did he?"

"No, only Archie knew," I replied, the guilt evident as I looked back up at Simon.

"But Archie didn't really know everything, did he? I asked him why he hadn't gone to get you sooner. He feels guilty about everything, but looking at how you ended up in hospital and comparing it to what he knew, I think you must have left out a few key details."

I bit down on my tongue and tried to stop myself from crying. A tear escaped as I opened my mouth to reply. "No, I told Archie Jason only hit me once. That was enough for Archie to lose his shit. I couldn't tell him any more. I didn't want to bother him, I'm not his problem. Archie came to my house—he shouldn't have done that, you don't know how much shit I got in …"

Sympathy was etched across Simon's face. "You need to stop thinking of yourself as a problem, you're an extraordinary person who went through more in your childhood than most people experience in their lives, and then you have whatever happened with him added to that. You're not a problem, you're a survivor."

Looking up at his light eyes, I realised that Archie must have found his safe space in Simon. It would take a lot for us to share any details about our childhood—the constant fear of what would happen when Dad had been drinking, the worry we all held for our mum who had struggled with her mental health, multiple hospital visits preventing her from being the parent we'd desperately needed. "Si, stop, please. I can't talk about this any more."

"You're going to have to when your big brother gets here. You know that, don't you?"

"Maybe I should cancel tonight with Ben, I don't really feel up to it now."

"Or you should invite him round instead, he may need a few blanks filled in about what's happened to you if he's hoping to pursue anything. It may also be good for you to have a big strong firefighter fighting your corner when Louis tries to drag you back to stay with him and keep you under lock and key."

Laughing together, we sank back down onto the bright orange sofa. "You might be right; do you have Ben's number? I deleted it." I hadn't wanted to have a moment of weakness and ask for his help. Stupid really.

"Yeah, he left it here when he first dropped you off, hold on." Simon reached down to the pile of magazines and passed me an old receipt with a number scribbled on it.

Sinking into the cushions of the sofa, I reached behind myself to pull my phone out of my back pocket. Saving his number into my phone, I opened up a blank text, pausing only to ponder what the night ahead would bring. I knew this wouldn't be easy, but my brothers were going to demand answers and I really didn't want to tell my story more than once. I didn't even want to tell it once, but I knew I'd have no choice.

Me: Hi Ben, it's Rosie Robinson, my brother is coming to see me so I won't be able to go out. You're welcome to come here instead and meet him, only if you want to. xo

Ben: Hi Rosie Robinson, that's a shame ... you sure you want me there?

Me: I do, I think I could use someone on Team Rosie. xo

Ben: I'm definitely Team Rosie. See you at seven, beautiful.

I held my phone close to my chest, my cheeks filling with heat. *Beautiful.*

"You're blushing. I take it the handsome fireman is coming round tonight?"

I picked up the cushion closest to myself and chucked it at a laughing Simon. "I'm going to my room." After standing up, I climbed back upstairs and threw myself across the bed. *Why do I have this reaction to Ben? I barely know him, and he definitely doesn't know me.* With my eyes shut tight it was easier to think about Ben and to picture his dark eyes. I started to drift into a peaceful slumber.

Ben

Arriving at seven on the dot, I looked up at number twelve as I lifted the brass knocker. Hoping to see Rosie, I was suddenly pushed back into the post of the porch. Instinctively I pushed back against the man who had charged at me, one hand in his shirt and the other fist lifting. "Who the fuck are you?" I snapped at my attacker.

"Whoa, whoa, whoa. Steady, boys, what is going on out here?" Archie's voice carried through to the outside. "Oh, for God's sake, Louis, put the man down."

"Is this him?" the man seethed through his clenched jaw.

Loosening my grip on his shirt, I lowered my fist. "You think I'm like her ex, don't you? That I'd do something like that to her?" I sneered at him, stepping away. He shared the same dark curly hair as Rosie. He was shorter than me but stocky. He could have landed a good punch if I had given him the chance.

"This is Rosie's friend, Ben. He was the one who picked her up on the ferry. Leave him be," Archie said.

Louis' eyes hadn't left me, but he slowly nodded, reaching out a hand to me. "Sorry, mate, I'm not thinking straight," he muttered, barely audible.

"Don't mention it." I gripped his hand firmly, silently giving him a warning to not try that with me again. Stepping past, I walked through the front door. Simon glanced over at me and ushered me to sit down.

I sat down beside him on the bright orange sofa. The walls were a dark navy, filled with mismatched photo frames—not my taste, but it felt warm and lived in. I busied myself looking up at the photos beside me, noticing one of a girl smiling playfully at the camera wearing a cap and gown, a graduation picture. Another showed a young Rosie smiling between two men who I now recognised as Louis and Archie. A smaller male and a woman stood proudly to the left of her. This woman had the same smile as Rosie, but her eyes looked sadder than Rosie's bright round eyes. Where the fuck were her parents? Who was looking out for her?

Louis and Archie joined us in the living room, sitting on the opposite navy sofa, staring back at me. This felt awkward. I had done a few 'meet the parents', but never a 'meet the brothers'. Was that what this was? Rosie had told me she wasn't ready for anything like this, but she had also asked me to be here tonight. Had she anticipated what had just happened? I smiled to myself knowingly—she wanted a distraction away from herself.

Rosie's smile stood out to me in various pictures across the room. One showed Rosie and Archie arm in arm by the Eiffel Tower. *She's been to Paris. I didn't know that.* Sighing to myself, I realised I really didn't know anything about her. I only knew she had escaped and, thanks to my police friend Rich, I knew how she had got here.

Silence continued in the quirky living room until I could hear light steps coming down the wooden staircase. I looked up as the door creaked open to see Rosie looking bemused at the sight of us all sat in an awkward silence.

"Um …" she started when Louis turned towards her, his jaw clenched.

"Sit. Down. Now."

It took everything I had to stop myself from grabbing him again and making him apologise to his sister. Rosie reacted quickly. She rushed round the coffee table and tactfully positioned herself between me and Simon. She looked down at her hands, not daring to look up at her brothers. I glared back at him.

"Sorry, Ro, I'm not angry at you," Louis said. "Please don't look at me like that, it's killing me seeing you like this. You're not yourself, what happened? Why are you here? They said you were covered in bruises and that you only had one bag with you. What's gone on, where's this Jason? Did he do this to you? Please tell me it wasn't him. Me and Rach knew something wasn't right. She's worried about you too, Ro."

Rosie let out a shudder at the mention of his name. Jason. At least now I had a name for the man I needed to kill.

She was picking at the fluff on her jeans, digging her nails into her leg, she was going to cut herself if she didn't stop. Lifting my hand gently, I placed it over her small hand, prying her nails from her jeans. She didn't fight me as I wrapped my fingers round hers and rested both our hands on the sofa between us. Remembering I was sat beside her, she looked up at me with a grateful smile. I could tell she needed me to be there for her in this moment. We were almost strangers, neither knowing anything about the other but both seeking comfort in being close in that moment.

She looked back at her brother and slowly shook her head, not knowing where to start.

"Ro, do you want me to start?" Archie offered, staring intently at his little sister. She took in a deep breath, then nodded, tears escaping her eyes.

I looked back at Archie, waiting to learn her story. I didn't know if I was ready to hear this, but if I wanted to get to know Rosie, I needed to know what she had been through.

"Well, Rosie rang me last year and told me that she needed my help to leave him. She told me he had hit her during an argument, and it wasn't the first time. She wanted to leave, but she didn't know how, so we made a plan that she would go to work and I would pick her up halfway through her shift and bring her back here. I went to the hospital, but her manager told me she hadn't turned up to work that day. I went to the house and Rosie told me to leave and that she had overreacted. I did try to make her come with me, but she refused. I wish I had dragged you out of there, Ro. I knew something didn't feel right."

Rosie was now using her other hand to dig her nails into her other thigh. Stretching behind her, I placed my arm across her shoulder and reached down to pick her hand up off of her jeans. I leant her body into me so she was able to nestle against me whilst I restrained her hands from injuring herself further. She was hurting enough listening to her brother. She didn't look at me whilst I cuddled her into me, but she didn't fight me either. Her shoulders dropped slightly as she relaxed into my side.

"So, you're telling me you fucking knew what was going on and you didn't get her out? You didn't tell us. You didn't tell me! You should have told me!" Louis started in on his brother. I glared up at him. Rosie's body tightened underneath me. She didn't need to be here for this.

"You weren't around, Louis, don't act as if you were checking in on her after she left," Archie retorted, lifting himself up slightly in his seat.

"Look, lads, this isn't helping anyone." I nodded my head towards their sister, who was now cowering beside me. Their eyes softened as they saw Rosie.

"Sorry, Rosie," Louis muttered under his breath.

"Rosie, I need to know how you got here, it's been bothering me since you arrived," Archie said apologetically, looking at his sister.

"I may be able to help fill in some of the gaps," I offered. Rosie looked up at me, brows furrowed, whilst the three others nodded quizzically. "I, uh, rang a police officer friend when Rosie turned up covered in bruises. She didn't want to speak to him, she freaked out at the hospital as soon as I told her he was coming to talk to her. She, uh ..." Remembering the night Rosie had had to be sedated, and knowing she wouldn't want anyone to know, I changed direction. "Anyway, I spoke to him that night. He was able to track how she got here, as we knew where she came from because of her uniform.

"Rosie left for work that morning, bringing Doug with her. She popped into work for ten minutes before leaving with a bag. He managed to pick her up on CCTV till she got to the cycle path beside the dual carriageway. From how long it took her to get to where we saw her on the ferry, I think she must have walked sixty fucking miles carrying that little dog."

I looked down at her and she gave a small nod. My chest hurt again when I thought about her walking in that condition, in that weather. Anything could have happened. Her brothers both looked equally pained to hear what I was sharing. I imagined that none of them liked the idea of her walking alone in that state.

"I spoke to her work," I said. "I know I shouldn't have, but one of the secretaries told me that Rosie had been off sick the week before she came in and quickly left. But I don't think you were sick, were you, Rosie?"

She shook her head. Still nestled into my arm, she turned her face slightly, hiding beside me.

"The hospital said most of her injuries were acute, which means they would have happened within a week of her arriving at hospital. They also said she had signs that she was dehydrated, starved, and restrained. He kept you in that house and tortured you, didn't he, Rosie?"

She let out a cry and leant forward quickly as she vomited down onto the rug in front of her. Standing her up, I rushed her through the corridor and led her to the bathroom. Helping her to kneel down, I stroked her hair out of her face and held it back with one hand as I used the other to rub her back as she continued to throw up.

"You're okay, you're safe now. He will never hurt you again," I promised her.

Simon poked his head round the door, looking down with sad eyes at his new sister. "Why don't you take her upstairs and get her settled, I'll deal with Dumb and Dumber in there." He motioned back to the living room, one hand on his other hip. "Thanks for being here, Ben."

I nodded and with one swift move I lifted Rosie up and carried her up the stairs towards an open door. Peering round the room, realising I had never been here before, I recognised the small bag she'd had when I'd first met her and the sausage dog curled up on a pile of clothes on the floor. God, she was messy. The room had clothes dumped on the floor, about seven empty water glasses on the side and three empty packets of strawberry laces. The TV was paused on an animated show. She had been watching *The Little Mermaid*. Lowering her to the double bed, I pulled back the duvet cover and tucked her in.

"Please don't leave me."

My heart sank at the sound of her timid voice. I walked over to the door, closed it gently. Leaving a lamp on, I turned off the main light. I slipped my shoes off and took off my jacket and sat back on the bed beside Rosie. I leant my head back against the wall and put my arm over her resting body. Knowing she wouldn't want to talk any more tonight, I lifted up the remote, which was wedged behind a pillow, and pressed play. I watched the cartoon fish and mermaid sing about having legs whilst Rosie drifted off to sleep.

CHAPTER 6
The Morning After

Ben

I woke the next morning to a warm snout sniffing up at me. Doug nestled into my armpit, using his legs to push a wedge between me and the body next to me. I reached my arm over and rested it gently around Rosie's shoulders. She sat up, quickly staring back at me. Our eyes locked and she let out a reassured sigh before lowering herself back down onto the bed, turning on her side and beaming up at me.

"That's cute," she said with a smirk, looking at the two of us. I stared appraisingly back at her. Before she fell asleep, I had been helping her up to bed after she'd vomited all over the floor and here she was the next morning trying to act as if nothing happened. I wondered if this was what she did—coasted through life denying anything that wasn't going right. I pursed my lips and nodded back at her, my lips slightly curled at the side, allowing her to pretend that this was normal.

Clearly not buying my reaction, she sat up and folded her arms across her small frame. "Look, you can go. No one asked you to stay. I'm fine, you don't need to worry about me," she exclaimed.

Ouch. If she wants to play these games, that's fine. "Actually, sweetheart, you asked me to stay, but I guess we're just pretending that nothing happened at all last night. I need to go to work anyway," I replied, matching the sting in my voice to hers. I manoeuvred the sleeping dog off of me. He opened his eyes for a moment, growled and then nestled back into the place my body had been.

I put my shoes back on and filled my pockets with my belongings, glancing at the time on my phone. 08:07. I needed to be in work soon. With one last glance around the room, I headed back through her bedroom door into the main house, avoiding looking at her sat sulking on the bed. *She asked me to leave, why is she sat there pouting?* Ignoring her bratty behaviour, I walked down the stairs and headed straight out of the front door. Reaching up, I pulled my hands through my hair as the fresh air hit me. *What am I doing? She clearly doesn't want me. I look pathetic.*

Rosie: I'm sorry, please come back.

I looked down at the screen in disbelief. I couldn't keep up with this. One minute she was pushing me away, the next she wanted me back. If I went back now, I'd just look even more pathetic, I'd look fucking weak. *This isn't me; I don't chase girls around.*

But if I didn't go, I didn't get to see her. I couldn't keep up with this. My life had been so much simpler before I saw her on that ferry.

Me: I can't, I have to work. We can talk later.

Already regretting my blunt response, I hit my palm against my forehead.

"Fuck!" I shouted out into the cold deserted street. I looked down at the time, then back towards the house I had departed.

I searched Jim's number and pressed dial.

"'Sup, boss?"

"All right, I'm going to be late. Can you cover?" I asked, my voice laced with desperation.

He laughed knowingly down the phone. "Guess your date went well, eh, boss?" he teased.

If only he knew. "Shut up. I'll see you later."

"Sure thing."

I hung up and turned on my heel, heading back through the door. Taking the stairs three at time, I was pathetically desperate to get back to her and apologise for walking away. My shoulders sagged as I found her hunched in a ball on the bed, hugging her knees and letting out quiet sobs. I rushed towards her, lifting her up and sitting her on my lap. I lifted my hand and grazed her face with the back of my knuckles as I wiped her tears away. I gently placed a kiss on her cheek. My lips met with the salt from her tears. I tightened my grip around her as she let out further cries.

"Shh," I whispered into her hair, my lips pressed firmly to the top of her head as I gently rocked her, "it's okay, I'm not going anywhere."

Her grip tightened on my arm as she repositioned herself so she could look up at me. "I'm sorry, Ben, I'm really sorry. I'm trying to not be a horrible person but I can't help it. I'm just nasty and evil and I'm horrible to everyone." The words rushed out of her, stumbling over her sobs as her body shook.

How can she think she's a horrible person? She really had no idea how everyone else saw her. I saw the way my team looked at her, like they wanted to protect her, admiration in their eyes at how strong she was. I saw how much her brothers cared for her like she was the most important person in the world to them, and I knew how I felt for her after only spending a short time together. I needed her as much as she needed me. She was mine.

"Shut up, Rosie," was all I could manage, trying to deflect her emotions and ignore her clear self-loathing.

She looked up at me, the sobs suddenly stopping as she smirked. "Shut up?" She jabbed me with her small fist into my arm. Not moving under her jab, I lifted her up slightly, laying her back on the bed as I rested my body gently on top of hers. Using my elbows to prop myself up either side of her head, I placed a gentle kiss onto her forehead, and then again onto her nose, lowering my face slightly to kiss her soft lips.

She looked back up at me through her wet eyelashes and watery eyes. I lowered my lips back down to hers, more forcibly this time. Her lips parted as my tongue linked with hers in a swift but passionate kiss. When I pressed my hips down, she made a small O with her mouth as I urged myself against her. Her eyes narrowed and her lips curled into a mischievous grin. She grabbed the back of my head, pushing her tongue into my mouth and forcing her body against mine. She reached up and pulled my jumper off over my head, my T-shirt coming with it. My hands were grazing her body, skimming up her side and brushing the side of her bra as I reached down again and lifted her chin up, deepening our kiss. Before I knew it, her T-shirt had come off, leaving her in her underwear.

She shuffled awkwardly underneath me as I stared at her body, her arms stretched across herself, hiding herself from me. I pulled her hands back and held them above her head, pinning her to the bed so I was able to take in the full sight beneath me. *Fucking hell.* Her waist was narrow, probably too narrow, but her olive skin swelled beneath her bra, her breasts just over a handful, spilling out over the edge of the lace. My tongue came out to wet my lower lip before I bit down as my eyes trailed to her hips, which came out further from her waist and curved in the best way, her body lifted above her round full behind. I wanted nothing more than to use her ass to pull her towards me and bury my face in her chest.

Noticing the look on my face, she giggled beneath me, biting her lip and wiggling her body, trying to press up against me again, looking for that friction. I stripped down to my boxers, my body still above her. In one move I lifted her body towards me, pressing myself further against her. She wrapped her legs around me. We brushed against each other, moving as one, my kiss deepening inside her mouth, my hands moving back down underneath her, grabbing onto her round behind. I desperately tried to restrain myself, to not allow this to go too far. She deserved better than a cheap make out session. The tears that had spilled weren't even dry.

I lifted my hand back around, skimming across her body as we kissed. My hand trailed over her breast, across the lace still hiding her from me, and rested around her neck, stopping only momentarily before I shifted my weight in an attempt to move my hand up beside her. She stopped instantly as my hand brushed her neck, her eyes wide and her body rigid. She looked at me with fear in her eyes, a frozen stare. Suddenly realising where my hand had rested, I pushed myself off the bed so that I was stood beside her.

"No, no, no, Rosie, I wasn't going to hurt you," I started, panicking at the icy stare on her face. "Shit, Rosie, stop! I'm not going to hurt you!" The desperation was clear in my voice. The only movement from her body was the increasing rise of her chest. Her lips parted and her eyes round. I hurriedly pulled my T-shirt back over my head and knelt back onto the bed.

"I'm sorry, it's too soon," I said weakly. She wasn't back in the room yet; her mind was still elsewhere, her eyes still vacant. I reached down and grabbed the T-shirt she had worn to bed and stretched it over her head, careful to not go anywhere near her neck. I lifted her hips up slightly as I pulled the T-shirt down, covering her back up. I tugged the duvet back onto the bed and over both of us as I held her, my grip tightening. I rocked her back and forth until her shoulders relaxed. She was asleep.

Twenty minutes later, I reached over to my jeans, which were still strewn across the floor, and with one hand I pulled my phone back out of my pocket, glancing at the time. 09:10. Shit, I really needed to go. I needed to leave, but didn't want to say goodbye. I also didn't want to leave without her knowing—the idea of her waking up and looking for me wasn't worth thinking about. Deciding it was better for her to know I had left, I shook her shoulder gently and kissed her cheek.

"I really have to go, but I'll come back and see you later," I whispered against her ear.

"You promise?" she said under her breath, not making eye contact with me.

"I promise."

She gave me a gentle squeeze and lifted her arm back up so I could clamber out of her bed.

I turned back around and gathered up my belongings, getting changed for the second time that morning.

"I'm really embarrassed," she said behind me, now sitting on the edge of the bed, her legs trembling.

I shook my head at her and smiled in what I hoped was a reassuring way.

"You don't talk much, do you?" she said, smiling back up at me.

"Only when I need to."

"Okay, well, maybe our next date we should talk more, instead of whatever happened last night," she said, her voice still laced with embarrassment. She could barely keep eye contact with me.

I smiled at her mention of our next date. I leant back down towards her, resting my hands either side of the bed where she was sat and dipping my head so I was level with her.

"Okay, we'll talk more on our *next date.*" I emphasised the words, making sure I enunciated each word clearly. She smiled up at me, giving me eye contact and letting out a small laugh, shaking her head.

I stood up straight, lifting my jumper over my head. "What are you doing today, darling?" I asked her.

"I might go buy a car," she replied casually.

"Why do you need a car?" She wasn't planning to leave, was she?

"Uh … to get around. I'll need to get a job if I want to stay here and I've never seen a bus here and everything is so far apart."

"Well, I can give you lifts, or you can use my car. I don't use it at work anyway." I was sounding desperate.

"That's sweet, but I really just want my own car."

"Well, I'll go with you. I'll make sure you don't get ripped off. The only dealership round here is Robbie's and he's a proper salesman, he'll flog you anything." I frowned at the idea of Robbie ripping off Rosie.

"Have some faith, Ben, it will be fine. I'll go in, find out about the deals and give you a call if it makes you feel better?"

"It does," I replied simply as I leant down, kissed her on the top of her head and walked quickly outside of number twelve before I convinced myself to return again.

CHAPTER 7

The Princess and the Salesman

Rosie

I got dressed quickly and took Doug outside into the garden to let him do his business, calling him back inside once breakfast was served. *Such a damn prince.*

Picking up my handbag, I glanced at myself in the full-length mirror. *Hmm, I guess this will have to do—this is as good as it's going to get.* I had messy hair and permanent bags under my eyes. I had dressed in skinny jeans and a thick fleece. Slipping on my faithful Converse, I headed out of the door. I pulled out my phone and opened up the maps app and searched for the car dealership. It was a twenty-seven-minute walk. *This is why I need a car, Ben.*

Putting my headphones in and blocking out the drone of traffic, I started my journey.

Twenty-three minutes later I was still listening to the same song on repeat for the fourteenth time. There was something comforting about the repetitive and predictable tune. When I looked down at the screen, my heart felt warm at the sight of the text messages dancing across my screen. Four unread messages. *Four!* This wasn't something I was used to; I was never allowed to have any messages before. It never ended well, so I'd discouraged anyone from ever contacting me.

> Simon: Hey lovely, movie night? I fancy *Pretty Woman!* xx

Me: You're on, anything for a bit of Richard. xo

Smiling down at the phone, I felt so lucky to have a new brother in my life. I already had a few, but I'd known from the first day I met Simon that we would be close. I loved him so much already. I clicked on the next message.

> Unknown: Hey doll, thinking about you. Don't forget your knight in shining armour over here. Ben said you were going to buy a car today, don't let Robbie convince you into a shit convertible.

Before I could begin to guess who this was, the phone buzzed again.

> Unknown: It's Trent. Ben reluctantly gave me your number when I threatened to pop round and see how you were doing. ;)

I laughed to myself—of course it was. Typing out a reply, I saved his number in my phone.

> Me: Thanks knight, I'll bear that in mind. I'm having a movie night tonight with Simon, but you're welcome to join us. *Pretty Woman?* xo

> My knight: Hell yes, Julia Roberts is a beauty. Laters, doll.

I clicked on the final messages.

Ben: I just gave Trent your number.

Ben: I didn't have much choice; he threatened to go over and see you tonight and that's not happening.

Me: No worries, but he's coming round tonight for movie night so you'll have to come join us.. xo

I realised I had been smiling down at my phone for most of the journey. It was a miracle when I looked up and saw the car garage with a big yellow sign across it: 'ROBBIE'S.'

Hmm, original name. Suppressing an eye roll, I walked through the double doors and looked around. A tall, lean man stood leaning against his desk, looking down at his phone, his long legs crossed almost arrogantly in front of him. "You must be Rosie?" He smiled up at me with a twinkle in his eyes.

He towered over me easily, his body slim but his suit straining against the muscles in his arms. His hair was dark, slicked back and shaved at the sides. He reminded me of a character in one of my books—a member of the mafia. Although his features were sharp, there was something familiar about his presence that put me at ease.

How did he know who I was? Was I sticking out too much? Did I need to stay home so no one else recognised me so I could stay safe? My mouth must have dropped open mid-thought, as he walked up towards me and lifted my chin up with one finger. Swatting his hand away, I scowled back at him with my hands on my hips.

"Don't worry, princess, I've already had your boyfriend on the phone threatening me to make sure I give you a fair deal on a *safe* car." He sneered back at me.

"I don't have a boyfriend," was all I could manage.

"Well, fuck, that makes this more fun," he said with a smile as he walked back towards his desk, pointing towards a chair opposite to encourage me to sit down. "Right, princess, let's get started. What's your budget?" He raised an eyebrow as he kept one eye on the computer screen in front of him.

Christ, straight to the money then. "Um, I don't know." I shifted uncomfortably in my seat.

"Look, princess, there's no point me showing you a load of cars you can't afford. Don't be shy about this." He leant forward in his seat.

"Okay, well, no more than ten." I had saved up a lot of money not being allowed out of the house alone for so many years.

Raising his eyebrows, he leant back in his chair, arms behind his head. "Impressive," he replied, standing from his chair, walking round the desk and ushering me to follow him without a second look. "I can work with that budget."

I chased behind him, struggling to keep up. His legs were much longer than mine and I still had a sharp, niggling pain in my ribs. Following him and his suit through the showroom, I stayed silent as he looked at the various cars.

"Ben said safe. The safest I have in your budget is this." He stopped and stood by a shiny oversized truck. I looked up at the car—it was massive. It had a bench front seat and three seats in the back. I liked it. It reminded me of a modern version of an old American pickup truck. "It's the safest, it's in your budget and if you get in an accident, you'll be doing the crushing rather than being crushed," he stated casually.

Amused, I shook my head.

"I think you'd look better in one of these." He gestured towards the small Barbie convertibles.

"I've been warned against these already, I'm afraid. Right, I'll go for the truck then, please." I straightened up, leaning slightly on the truck as I felt another wince of pain in my side.

Robbie looked at me, tilting his head. "You all right there, princess?"

"Yes, fine. Can we go back to the desk and sit down so I can buy this monster?"

"Sure …" He walked over to me and linked my arm through his as we walked back over to his desk. I smiled up at him, thankful for this small gesture. He lowered me in the seat, turned back around the desk, sat across from me, and looked up at me with pensive eyes. "You all right? Want me to call your non-boyfriend?"

"Nah, I'm fine. I just need to buy this car and drive back home."

He shrugged in defeat. "Cash or card?" he asked with a bored expression as he reached for the card machine.

"Cash." I lifted a handful of cash from my bag. His eyes opened wide as he saw the bundles of cash in my small fist.

"Lucky I ask no questions about how I receive payments, princess. Does your man know you walk around with that much cash on you?" He took the cash and started counting.

"I thought you said no questions?" I raised my eyebrows at him, returning the remaining cash into my bag.

He laughed and mimicked fastening a zip across his mouth. He wrote me out a receipt, disappeared into the back room and returned with two sets of keys, a car manual and a business card. "Just in case you needed anything, princess," he added as I stashed the card with his number in my bag.

"Thank you." He was actually all right once you saw past the salesman chatter.

Moments later I climbed up into the truck. Robbie stood behind me and lifted me into the truck with his big hands wrapped around my waist.

"Please call me when you get back home, princess. I'm a little bit worried about you."

"You don't know me, so don't worry, and stop calling me 'princess'," I snapped back at him, reaching to shut the door in his face. *Bit mean, but I'm over all the pitying looks.*

Robbie stopped me by placing his hands over the keys in the ignition. "Look, princess, if I let you drive home when you're in that much pain and you don't make it, I'll probably get into trouble with your man and his gang," he said, eyes now glued onto his shuffling feet, his overconfident demeanour fading.

"How many times do I have to tell you that I don't have a man!" I raised my voice back at him, now frustrated at him stopping me from leaving. *Why does everyone feel they need to look after me?* "And for the record, he's not in a gang, he's a fireman. They're his team, not his gang." I cringed as I said the word 'gang'.

Robbie looked at me. "How long have you known Ben, princess?"

"Long enough." I reached again for the door handle. His body was wedged in between the door and the car. He took a gulp, his Adam's apple bobbing, and gritted his teeth.

"Just be careful. Get to know the company you keep a bit better." And with that he slammed the door shut.

I slumped back down onto the now-heated seats and shook my head, snapping myself out of my thoughts. What did he mean, be careful? Was he trying to suggest Ben was in a gang? Ben had been right about Robbie. "Asshole," I muttered under my breath.

I drove out of the forecourt and headed straight towards the fire station, wanting answers.

Pulling up to the station, I was met with a chorus of cheers because of the new wheels I was driving. Trent came out running towards the car, reached for the handle and lifted me out. "Whoa, doll, this is a tank! You sure you can manage it?" he asked, still holding onto me, dragging me round with him as he circled the car.

On our second lap of the engine I noticed that Ben had joined the laughing crowd. I stopped suddenly in front of him. "What are you laughing at? No fires today then, I'm guessing?"

He stared up at me, his eyes narrowing, clearly not impressed with being asked questions in front of his team. *Or his gang?*

He folded his arms across his broad chest. "You want to start that again, sweetheart?"

Realising I was still in bitch mode from my time with Robbie, I shook my head, trying to reset my attitude. "Sorry, hello." I stood on my tiptoes to kiss him on the cheek. He pulled me towards him and turned his head slightly so my kiss landed on the corner of his mouth. He wrapped his arm possessively round me as he guided me over to my new car, ignoring the wolf-whistles and laughs from the rest of the firefighters.

"Want to show me your new car?" he asked as he looked down at me, eyes softer since our kiss. I nodded shyly as he turned to the rest of the men. "Back to work," he said calmly, and they all retreated into the station without argument.

Ben watched as I tried to lift myself into the truck, pausing as I lifted my leg onto the step. "How did you even get into this? Are you sure you can drive it?"

My ginormous truck was a bit ridiculous, but I liked it. "Well, Robbie lifted me in. But I will be fine once this is better," I said frustratedly, pointing at my ribs.

"He lifted you in?" Ben asked, narrowing his eyes once again, stepping closer towards me. Biting down on my lip so I couldn't incriminate Robbie further, I stared at my feet. "He touched you?"

Recognising this as anger, I started to panic. *What if he hurts me?*

I had gone quiet and withdrawn, my eyes plastered on the ground. Ben's voice softened. "Sorry, Rosie, it's okay. I'm not mad at you. It's Robbie, he pisses me off."

"He said you were in a gang," I blurted out. *Shouldn't have said that.*

"He what?" Ben asked as he lifted me into the truck so I was sat with my legs facing him. He leaned his arm against the edge of the car, his hand running through his hair, clearly upset. Realising I had dropped poor Robbie in it, I remained silent. Robbie was only worried about me.

"He's talking shit, Rosie; I'll go see him tonight." Ben looked away, as if that were final and the conversation was done.

Sitting back in my chair, I pulled the door shut. Immediately Ben wrenched it back open. "Seat belt." He didn't give me a chance to respond— he reached across me, pulled my seat belt with me, and plugged it in.

I grabbed his hand as he pulled the seat belt back across me. He looked up at me, eyes softening as they met mine. "Please just drop it. I don't care what he said. I just don't need any more dramas, I want to be happy. I bought a car," I added quietly, feeling embarrassed about how dumb I sounded.

"You did, sweetheart. I'll drop it for now, but if he continues, I get to speak to him. Deal?"

Smiling back up at Ben, I nodded. "Deal."

"Love it when you smile."

"Kiss me then?" I asked him through my smile. He leant down and kissed me, pressing his lips hard against mine and stroking my face with the palm of his hand, tactfully avoiding my neck.

With a wave, I drove back out of the entrance to the station and onto the main road. I looked into my rear-view mirror and saw him watching as I disappeared into the traffic.

CHAPTER 8

'She Rescues Him Right Back'

Ben

Watching Rosie drive away in her new truck, I felt proud of how pleased she felt that she had bought herself a car. I waited till she was out of sight before turning back around and heading for my office. "Jim, Mike, Trent. With me," I snapped as I marched past them. They stood up quickly, recognising the tone in my voice, and followed me back to my office.

Sitting behind the desk, I looked at the three of them stood in front of me. "Robbie told Rosie that I'm in a *gang*." I paused, waiting for their reaction.

Jim sank down into the chair in front of me. "Little shit. What did you say to her?"

"I said I wasn't, and that's how I'd like to keep it. She's been through enough; she doesn't need to know what we've done here too. She couldn't handle it; she's so fucking fragile." There was a clear warning tone in my reply.

"Ben, if you want to start something real with this girl you should be honest with her. She's more resilient than you're giving her credit for. Look what she's gone through." Mike always was the voice of reason.

"No. We haven't had to be active in a long time and I don't plan on going back to those ways. Not now I have Rosie to think about."

"Well, you're the boss," Trent said, standing behind me and glaring at Mike.

"Fine," Mike said, slightly under duress.

"If we have to tell her, we will, and I'll deal with it. But not now, please. Trust me, she's not ready for any more," I said, now pleading with my team.

"We trust you, boss," Jim said. Mike and Trent nodded their heads in agreement. "What do we do about Robbie then?" Jim asked.

"We do nothing."

"What? Why?" Trent asked.

"She asked me not to and I gave her my word we wouldn't." This was my decision, but I still couldn't look directly at my team.

"You are so whipped," Trent said in between laughs.

I shook my head, joining in with his laughter. *He's right, I am.* I ran my hand through my hair and down my face, my touch skimming along the scar across the side of my face—a scar that served as a constant reminder of the night that had started it all, the night where I'd lost everything, including myself.

The last few weeks I had started to feel more alive. Rosie landing in my life the way she had had brought about a new purpose, a reason to change my ways.

The rest of the shift was fairly uneventful. We were called to a road traffic collision to pull a girl out of her semi-crushed tiny car. She looked the same age as Rosie ... or so I thought. We'd never talked about age. I didn't know when Rosie's birthday was. I really didn't know much about her. Shaking my head, I felt grateful knowing Rosie was safe driving around in a monster truck.

We got back to the station, had showers, got changed, then Trent and I left to see my girl.

We pulled up outside number twelve and headed towards the door, laughing at each other—two grown men were so charmed by this girl that we were going to watch *Pretty Woman* at her house with her brother and his husband.

Knocking on the door, we were greeted by an amused Archie. "You both been roped into movie night too?" he teased, welcoming us into the house. We kicked off our boots and headed through the open door of the living room. The sofas had been repositioned, so they were facing the big TV hung on the gallery wall. Simon knelt on the floor, setting up the TV sound. Louis sat in the only armchair, only looking up from his phone to nod at both me and Trent. Trent headed over to introduce himself to Louis and shake his hand. Trent then sat on the navy sofa, leaning back and getting comfortable.

"Where's Rosie?" I asked, noticing she wasn't in the room.

"I'm in here!" she called through the open doors. I followed the direction of her voice and found her reaching down into the oven and pulling out a dish of what looked like enchiladas. My stomach grumbled at the smell.

"Hungry then?" She smiled at the noise, swatting my stomach gently. She carried the enchiladas back through from the kitchen and placed them onto the coffee table. She then proceeded to place down serving spoons, plates, cutlery, and a bowl of nachos loaded with guacamole and salsa. "Everyone happy with beer?" she called over her shoulder. Her question was met with a chorus of yeses.

She headed back into the kitchen and I followed her in to help her carry the drinks. Blocking her with my body, I stopped her and pulled her in for a quick kiss, then held her tightly against my chest. She visibly relaxed as I wrapped my arms around her.

Letting go, I reached past her and lifted six bottles of beer out of the fridge. Rosie picked up a bottle opener and followed me back into the living room. Archie and Simon were now sat on the orange sofa. We passed out the beers as we let the food cool slightly. Rosie headed over to the navy sofa Trent was sat on and went to sit down next to him. I scooped my arm round her waist and pulled her back down onto my lap and away from Trent. Louis stared at us, but I ignored him. I didn't care what he thought about this. She was my girl.

We all dug in to the delicious Mexican feast Rosie had made. Our groans of enjoyment filled the silence as we tasted the food. Rosie looked around at us all, her plate empty, smiling at her satisfied guests.

"You are eating?" I nudged her, pointing at her empty plate.

"I ate loads whilst I was cooking, I'm fine for now," she replied as she put down her plate and lifted her beer to her lips.

Archie and Simon shared a look. Why did I sense this was something about which they were worried? Deciding to let it go and pick my battles, I placed my plate down and pulled her into me. "That was amazing, thank you, sweetheart," I whispered into her ear. She rested her head against me. Curling my arm around her waist, I placed my hand against her ribs, where she winced again at the contact. "When do you go back for your next check-up?" I asked her quietly, knowing she wouldn't want anyone to worry.

"I went today, actually," she replied.

"Why didn't you tell me? I would have gone with you."

"It's fine, Ben," she retorted, and I didn't want to push her. We all sat back and watched the film in silence. I looked down to see Rosie nestled in my arms—she had fallen asleep.

I woke her up. Quoting the film, I whispered in her ear, "'And she rescues him right back.'" She grinned up at me, a sleepy smile, before closing her eyes again. It was true. Life felt brighter with Rosie in it.

"Do you believe in happily ever afters, Rosie?" Unsure where that question had come from, I watched hesitantly as her eyelids fluttered as she considered her response.

"I try not to let myself, Ben. If you don't dream you can't get disappointed."

I let her fall back asleep, not wanting to push that thought process further.

After Richard Gere had picked up Julia Roberts in his posh car, Trent let out a loud, exaggerated yawn and stretched. He checked his watch, then stood up quickly. "Shit. Didn't realise how late it was, I better get back to Holly."

"Molly." I coughed, reminding him of his current flame's name.

"Yeah, Molly, Holly, whatever. She's at mine. You ready to go?" he asked me, staring down at the now-asleep Rosie in my lap.

I reached down uncomfortably into my pocket and pulled out my keys. "Take my car, I'll stay here and take Rosie's truck in the morning."

"Cheers, pal, have fun. Nice to meet you, mate," he said, turning towards Louis, who was burning holes in the side of my head with his eyes. Louis looked up at him and nodded, stood up and left the room without another word.

"He's chatty," Trent joked, scowling at the back of Louis as he left.

Simon and Archie laughed with Trent as they saw him out of the house. Archie bent down to start cleaning up the empty plates and dishes.

I went to lift Rosie out of my arms to stand up and help when Archie stopped me. "No, let her sleep. She looks peaceful."

I nodded gratefully, shifted slightly, and stood with Rosie in my arms. "Night," I called as I carried her up the stairs and headed towards her room. Twice in a row I'd carried Rosie to bed. I could get used to this.

I lifted an exhausted Rosie onto her bed, stripped off her outer clothes, took off my T-shirt and lowered it over her head—it swamped her. I unclipped her bra under her T-shirt, removing it so she could lie back comfortably. Tucking her underneath the comforter, I took off the rest of my clothes, stripping down to my boxers. Before I turned off the light, I placed her phone on charge. Getting into her small bed with a smile on my face, I held her close in my arms, her heart beating against mine.

CHAPTER 9

Tall Cop, Small Cop

Rosie

Loud thuds at the door disturbed my daydream. I was sat relaxing on the sofa at number twelve pretending to look for jobs. Really, I had been watching the latest episode of a reality dating show and feeling envious of the sunshine location.

As I approached the door, the banging started up again. "All right, I'm here!" I shouted. Opening the door, I was greeted by two police officers in full uniform. My heart skipped a beat—this uniform only reminded me of my ex. The instant feeling of fear flooded my body as my legs started to shake. I stared blankly at them, unable to speak.

"Miss Robinson?" the taller out of the two asked. I nodded my head, still unable to find my words. "We need to bring you in to talk to you. You've been reported as missing and I think it's best we discuss this further with you at the station."

"Well, I'm not missing. I'm an adult and I'm choosing to be here, so thank you for your concern, but I'm okay." I smiled, trying to use all my knowledge as a shield of armour. I hadn't agreed to talk to the police and wasn't willing to do so now.

"I understand, miss, but we've been told to bring you in, so I think it's in your best interest to come have a chat and we can smooth everything out," the shorter one said, not leaving me any room to object.

Sensing it would be beneficial to comply, I nodded. "Okay, well, let me go get my bag."

The shorter police officer had his dirty boot wedged, blocking my attempts to close the door. Hooking my bag off the stairs covertly, I ran upstairs to my bedroom to feign collecting my bag. Instead, I typed out a hurried text to the one person I knew would help me.

Me: Ben, police are here and say I have to go to the station, can you meet me there?? xo

I didn't wait for a reply as I put my phone on silent and headed down the wooden stairs. I could feel my bag vibrating, but I didn't let on to the police officers. Faking a smile, I followed them to their police car, where they encouraged me into the back seat.

This wasn't the first time I'd been in a police car; my ex had called the police on me before. It didn't feel any easier. My pulse was racing as I tried to pretend to be interested in the scenery, staring fixedly out of the window at the blur of green and blue.

When we arrived at the police station, the surly officers led me into an isolated room filled with soft cushy chairs. I assumed they were an attempt to make people feel comfortable and safe. I sat down in the chair closest to the door. I had learnt this in my role as a nurse—stay close to the exit when you were having a difficult conversation. Nothing worse than being trapped in a room with an angry family. I placed my bag on my lap protectively and smiled up at the officers, who had sat across the stained pine coffee table from me.

"Drink, love?" the one I had labelled as Tall asked.

"No, thank you," I replied in my sickly sweet, compliant voice.

"Right, your boyfriend has reported you as missing and he's very, very worried about you, young lady," the one I'd labelled as Small said in a patronising tone.

"I don't have a boyfriend." I sighed. "Me and my ex-partner split up, we had a different outlook on life, it didn't work out." I stood my ground, making every effort to not scoff.

Tall piped up, "Love"—clearly he was the 'good cop'—"we know you presented to hospital with lots of nasty injuries. We managed to get copies of your medical records. Seems as if you told a few fibs. You didn't get beaten up, did you? You fell down the stairs and got a bit disorientated."

My blood started to boil as I struggled to stay calm, letting out that pent-up scoff. "Officer, how did you get access to my medical records? I am fully versed on healthcare law and know that I should have provided some level of consent for those." I plastered my fake smile onto my face and tilted my head at both Tall and Small. *Gotcha there.*

"Your boyfriend is willing to keep this to himself, of course … if you are?" Small piped up again. Clearly, he wanted this finished. Bad cop.

"I don't have any charges against anyone," I answered honestly.

"I know, but I'm sure your boyfriend would appreciate nothing coming up at all."

"I'm sure he would. Tell me, officers, do your managers know you're having this conversation or are you just trying to get intel for your buddy?" I asked, dropping any niceties I had just shown. I was beyond pissed.

Small stood up, reached directly behind me for an envelope so I could smell his cheap aftershave mixed in with stale cider. I knew what he was doing—he was trying to intimidate me. He emptied the envelope in front of me. Pictures of myself that had been taken by medical photography in the hospital appeared. My body had been covered head to toe in bruises. Oh, shit, I hadn't seen these before.

"See? These could easily be caused by tripping down the stairs. You had a few drinks?" Small stared directly at me, his shit-coloured eyes glistening. "However, a stab wound is harder to hide, isn't it? Only one possible mechanism for a stab wound, isn't there?"

Fuck. In an act of self-defence, I had stabbed my ex in the leg with a nearby screwdriver when he'd last tried to rape me. It hadn't stopped him.

My face paled and my heart started fluttering, my body going into panic mode. I leaned forward, tears spilling down my face. The two officers looked chuffed at my reaction, knowing they had something on me, when the door flung open. I saw a man in a suit and stood behind him was Ben. Letting out a huge exhale, I looked up and thanked whoever might be up there looking down on me.

"What the hell is going on in here?" Suit Man barked across the room. His voice was commanding enough to cause Tall and Small to cower in their seats. "Who gave you idiots clearance to be talking to her? Evans, you know you're on your last warning and this is what you decide to do?" He turned towards me after scolding the smaller of the two, glancing at the coffee table, scanning the photos before returning his eyes to mine. His eyes softened as he scooped the pictures back into the envelope, slipping them inside his suit jacket. "Rosie, my name is Rich. I'm one of the detective sergeants here. I'm sorry for any distress this has caused you. I will ensure everyone is dealt with accordingly." He glared back towards Small and Tall, who were looking down at their feet like two schoolboys caught in an embarrassing act. "Are you okay?"

I nodded, but my face gave me away as new tears spilled down my cheeks. Rich looked over me to Ben, still stood at the door. Ben's fists were clenched, his brows pulled together across his reddening face. "Take her home," Rich said.

Ben walked round to me and lifted me out of my seat, holding my bag as he used one arm to guide me out of the station. As we walked through the corridor I could hear Rich screaming at the two officers for their gross misconduct. It sounded as if they had been paid to bring me in—it wasn't hard for me to guess who was behind this.

The background noise of the station had quietened, as if I had gone underwater. I couldn't concentrate. All I could think about was that *he* had found me. He knew where I was and I wasn't safe on this island any more and I had been an idiot to think I was.

Ben drove me home in an uncomfortable silence. "I hate to do this, but I have to go to work. I want to be here with you, but I can't get out of this." He looked upset, the palm of his hand slamming down on the steering wheel. "Do you want to talk about it?" he offered.

I shook my head quickly. "It's fine, Ben, thank you for picking me up."

When I turned to leave, Ben leant over me and pulled my door shut. "Rosie, I promise those idiots will get what they deserve. I know you don't want to talk about it, but when you do, I'm here. I'm always here for you. I've texted Archie—he's inside and will spend the evening with you. Please stay in tonight." His strong hand rubbed the back of his neck, where he was holding tension.

"Okay, sorry I'm such a burden." My head hung in shame; my eyes stung. Calling Ben to rescue me again had been a mistake.

Ben shook his head, pursed his lips, then pulled me in for a sideways hug before I exited the truck and walked back through number twelve. My body shook as the adrenaline that had kept me together vanished and I instantly melted into a big mess.

Ben

Pacing my office, I waited for Rich to answer. When he did, I didn't give him a chance to greet me before I leapt down his throat. "Can I assume they'll be dealt with?"

"Consider it done. Sorry, mate, someone's obviously got to them." Rich sounded apologetic and pissed off, but I didn't care.

"Where did they get those pictures?"

"Turns out that ex of hers has a few strings he was able to pull. Paid off two of my officers to bring her in. Unfortunately, some strings were also pulled to get access to her medical information. Turns out my officers filled in the medical record request form under the guise of acting on behalf of Rosie. I'm dealing with it, trust me, Ben," he urged. "Let me know if she does want to press charges, she can with that evidence."

I knew the photos were the evidence he was referring to. "Anyone pulls anything like that again with her and I'll deal with them myself. And hide those fucking pictures, keep them safe," I warned before hanging up the phone.

CHAPTER 10

Tequila and Torment

Rosie

The internet at number twelve was rubbish, so Ben let me use his office to continue my job search, plus it was a bonus to be surrounded by good-looking firefighters. It should be so easy for me to get a job, I was a qualified nurse, surely people were crying out for nurses!

Letting out a huge, exaggerated sigh, I slumped back into the leather office chair as Ben entered the room. He looked at me and raised one of his dark eyebrows. Leaning forward, I slammed the lid on the laptop. "I can't find any local nurse jobs," I said on an exhale.

He planted a soft kiss on the top of my head. "Good."

I stood up to face him. "What do you mean good? I can't be a freeloader forever." I knew my brothers didn't mind, but I did.

"I don't want you working as a nurse here, it's too easy for Jason to find you," Ben said without looking at me. Shocked by his response, I reached out and grabbed his hand, tugging slightly, wanting him to explain what he meant. "He knows you're a nurse, he knows you're on the island, so it's not long before he starts calling round and asking where you are."

Did Ben also think Jason would come after me? I remained silent and slightly pissed off at the audacity he had asking me not to go back to nursing. As if I needed his permission.

"Sweetheart, I want him to come here so I can kill him, but if you're working, I'll never be able to concentrate because I'll be thinking about you. You don't need to work, but if you want to, please think about something else … for now."

Sulking slightly with my arms crossed, I begrudgingly nodded in agreement. What else would I do? All I'd ever been was a nurse. Straight from school I'd done my nurse training, and it had been my only escape from my relationship back home, working long shifts and often signing up for doubles and extra shifts to avoid my reality. Maybe I didn't need to avoid my reality any more. Still, it wasn't Ben's decision. Having my choices taken from me felt suffocating.

Feeling as if my identity had been stripped from me, I walked straight out of the office and in the direction of my truck. I felt Ben try to pull me back. Turning, I stared back at him, tears in my eyes. "Let go of me."

He didn't let go, instead he tightened his grip on my wrist.

"Please just let me go, I need some time," I said calmly, trying to wriggle my wrist free from his strong grasp.

"Rosie, calm down and get back to my office, we can talk about this."

"There's nothing left to talk about. You've already decided for me. I need some space; this is getting too much."

He stared down at me with hurt in his eyes as he dropped my wrist and allowed me to walk away. Visibly shaking with anger and frustration, I climbed back into the truck. I didn't need another man trying to coerce me. I'd thought I could be free here, but I suddenly felt more trapped than ever. Pulling out my phone, I dialled quickly.

"Go for Robbie." His cheery tone rang through the speaker.

"Uh, hi, Robbie, it's Rosie. Um …"

"Princess? Is that you?"

"Yes, sorry to bother you. I just wondered if you fancied going for a drink?"

"You asking me out, princess?"

"No."

"Ah, well, I'm at the pub anyway, the Swan. See you in a minute." He hung up.

Searching a map app for the pub , I pressed go and followed the blue arrows.

I pulled up at the Swan six minutes later, parking my car further away so I could have an easy parking space. I jumped out and walked towards the entrance. This pub was cute, built from old stone, and the walls were covered in wisteria. There was bunting mixed in with festoon lights above my head, lighting the path forward towards the tequila. A bell chimed above my head as I pushed open the wooden door. A few people looked towards the door. I dipped my head automatically.

"Princess, over here," Robbie called across the crowds. I smirked at his goofy smile, paired with his big hands waving. He looked like a Disney character.

Robbie was lanky; he looked as if he had been stretched. He was wearing one of his work suits without the tie and had his collar open. He was stood with another man in a similar suit with his hair slicked back and a pearly white smile. Stood next to him was a small petite woman with blonde hair perfectly straightened and styled behind her back. They both smiled at me, welcoming me to their table.

Robbie pulled back the empty chair, allowing me to sit with them. Robbie went to the bar, then returned to the seat next to me and handed me a pint of beer. "I took a guess," he said with a shrug.

The corners of my mouth turned up at the cold beer in front of me. "Perfect, thank you." Lifting the beer to my lips, I let out a small moan of appreciation at the taste of the amber liquid slipping too easily down my throat. My shoulders relaxed. I placed the beer back down and looked at the other smiling faces round the table.

"Princess, this is Joey and his girlfriend Miranda. Joey works with me and Miranda works at the bank." He turned back to his friends and continued. "Guys, this is Princess, apparently her real name is Rosie and apparently her boyfriend isn't Ben Bradley."

Miranda laughed sympathetically as I scowled at Robbie's introduction. "Hi, Rosie, nice to meet you." She smiled sweetly at me. I smiled back. It was nice to meet some normal people.

The night was fun. We ordered round after round of beer until Joey came back to the table with tequila shots. Four beers and three shots later I found myself sat on the toilet, steadying myself against the cubicle walls. I pulled out my phone to check the time … shit, eleven missed calls and five unread messages. I looked at the missed calls—seven from Ben, two from Trent, one from Archie and the last from an unknown number.

Fumbling my phone in my drunk hands, I opened my messaging app, feeling anxious about what might be there.

Ben: I'm sorry. We can talk about the nursing thing. I'll come round tonight after work. x

Ben: I'm at yours. Simon says you haven't been home yet.

Ben: Answer the fucking phone.

My mind spinning, I giggled at 'Simon says'. I skipped through the other messages, leaving them quickly, knowing full well he would see I had opened them.

Louis: Heading home today, I'll be back next week. Call me if you need anything, love you. xx

I smiled at the sweetest message he had ever sent me. I did love him too, even if he was annoying and the world was spinning right now.

Unknown: Where are you?

Assuming it was one of Ben's Merry Men, I replied.

Me: Tell Ben I'm fine. I'm at the Swan with Robbie and his friends, they're fun and they love tequila, which means I love tequila too. Night night. xo

Dropping my phone back into my bag, I wandered back through to the crowded pub. I strolled over to our table and sat back down with my new friends, laughing as I almost missed my chair. We spent the rest of the night laughing, joking, and talking about everything and anything.

I checked the time on my phone again. It was getting late, and I started to wonder about how I'd be getting home when my phone started to ring again. Ben's name flashed across the screen. Robbie was leaning over me and gave me a tight smile. "You may as well get it over and done with, princess, he's not going to get calmer."

Wise words for a man who looked like he had three sets of eyes. I swiped across the screen and tentatively lifted the phone to my ear. Before I got the chance to speak, I heard a grumpy Ben.

"Where are you?"

"I told you; I texted you," I said, my words slurring in reply.

"You didn't and you're drunk, where are you?"

"The Schwan," I garbled back.

"Don't move. Who are you with?"

"My new friends and Robbie."

"And Robbie?" Robbie laughed out loud. "Rude!"

My ear snapped back to the phone at the sound of a growl. "Put him on," Ben said calmly.

"Robbie, it's for you." I shoved the phone into Robbie's hand.

He lifted the phone hesitantly to his ear. I listened to the one-sided conversation. "Okay, yep. I'll wait with her. I said I wouldn't leave her. Bye." He hung up the phone and chucked it into my bag.

"Am I in trouble?" I asked Robbie, looking up into his agitated face.

"Nah, princess, you're fine. Come on, I'll wait with you outside." He stood beside me, pulling my chair back and helping me up. He reached around and linked my arm around his and steered me towards the door.

We stood outside in the fresh air waiting for Ben to arrive. I felt a sense of impending doom as we stood there in the cold empty car park waiting for him. My eyes snapped up from the car I was focusing on as I felt someone else's presence. The hairs on the back of my neck tipped up and a cold sheet of ice came over me.

"Rosie."

I turned around, looking in the direction of the familiar voice, and that was when I saw Jason.

His signature rings glinted, tormenting me under the shine of the festoon lights. I automatically winced, bringing myself back to the feeling of that metal connecting with my skin. His light hair was cut short, the vein above his temple prominent, his lips tipped up to showcase his toothy sneer. He was stocky and well built, not as tall as Ben, but still able to tower over and overpower me. His thighs were thick from years of rugby, his feet wearing his signature steel-toed boots. I couldn't pull my eyes away from the rings on his right hand. He looked down at his hand and let out a chuckle, swinging his arm forward and flexing his hand. It felt as if the blood had drained from my body. My legs wobbled and buckled beneath me as I fell to the ground in front of Robbie.

"Princess? What's going on?" Robbie looked back again at the man approaching us. "Who the fuck are you?" Robbie shouted at him, still trying to pull me up from the ground.

Ben's truck spun into the car park with a loud squeal of tyres and stopped directly between us and man who had haunted my dreams. Ben jumped out and circled his truck, squaring up to the stranger in front of us. "You fucked up coming here."

Jason looked up at him and let out a loud laugh, glancing towards me, still cowering on the ground. The all-too-familiar smile spread across his face again, causing me to recoil further. He slowly turned back towards the main road and disappeared into the darkness.

Ben

"Uh, bro, want to fill me in?" Robbie asked me as I joined him beside Rosie, who was frozen with fear on the cold damp ground. She was the only thing stopping me from running after her ex. "Who was that?" Robbie asked again, filling the silence.

"Just help me get her in the truck, I'll give you a lift home," I replied as I tried to scoop Rosie off of the ground, the alcohol in her system making it so much harder. Rosie's phone fell as we lifted her up and sat her down in the back of the truck. Robbie jumped into the back and lifted her body so she was sat up straighter against the window. Her phone was flashing on the ground. I picked it up and opened the unread message.

Unknown: I'm back, babe, and I won't let you go this time.

I scrolled up to the previous message where Rosie had told him where she was. The alcohol had skewed her judgement. She needed to be more fucking careful. Feeling a unexpected pang of fear, mixed with an intensified rage, I realised it was too easy for him to get to her. I needed to keep her safe. Seeing her reaction to him broke me—he scared her more than anything in the world.

Climbing into the driver's seat, I glanced in my mirror and saw Robbie sat in the back middle seat, propping a drunk and shocked Rosie up against the window. We couldn't go back to her brother's; I couldn't risk him finding her again. I kept glancing to Robbie's hand on her shoulder. *Don't hit him. Don't hit him.*

"Can we stay with you tonight?" I hated asking him a favour. He was such a smarmy prick and he had his hands on my girl.

"Yeah, of course that's fine, you know that. Was that who she was running from then?"

My mouth opened to ask what he meant. I didn't need to ask. He responded. "It was obvious to me, she paid for the car in cash, mate, I could tell something wasn't right."

As I tried to focus on the road, for the first time in my life I was completely unable to control my thoughts. If I hadn't got there in time, her ex would have taken her from me.

We pulled into the garage next to the flats where Robbie lived and parked up. I jumped out quickly, rushing towards the back of the truck to help Robbie lift Rosie out of the car. Her eyes were frozen in that watchful, worried stare and her body stiff, still clearly in shock. We stood side by side, propping her up, walking into the lobby and getting her into the lift. We went up to level six and walked towards Robbie's flat. He pulled out his keys and began to unlock the door. This took longer than usual, I imagined due to the tequila I could smell on the pair of them. He eventually pushed open the door and we piled in.

I rested Rosie on the sofa and Robbie handed me a couple of blankets. Placing a pillow beneath her head and tucking her in with the blanket, I placed a cushion underneath her in case she rolled off in the night.

"Night then," Robbie called as he headed into the bedroom. Waving him off, I stared across the room at Rosie, hoping she'd wake up the next morning out of this catatonic state.

I wracked my brain to think about what we could do. Her ex had found her. It hadn't taken him long—I'd known he would be after her, it was such typical behaviour from these perpetrators. I needed to get her away, keep her safe.

Me: Rosie's ex has turned up on the island, he saw us outside of the Swan and I imagine he's still here as there's no more ferries till the morning. Find him and make sure he leaves before I kill him.

Jim: I'll call Rich and get on it now.

Mike: Is Rosie okay?

Me: She's okay. I think she's in shock, but she's not safe any more and she won't be with him here on the island.

Trent: I'll get rid of him.

Me: Keep me updated.

Jim: Rich has already traced him and picked up his plates. I'm going
down there now. I'll pick you boys up.

Me: Thank you.

Trent: Anything for Doll face.

I finally put down my phone, feeling reassured that they would handle it. We knew how to convince people to give us our own way. I wanted to kill her ex, but I wouldn't give him that easy exit and satisfaction. The idea that I would be taken away from Rosie and locked up also deterred me.

Readjusting the cushions, I rested my head back against the armchair, staring at Rosie. She had rolled onto her back, her eyes wide open and fixated on the ceiling, tears streaming from her eyes. I left her on her sofa, pretending I hadn't seen, not wanting to make things worse. Every part of me wanted to go with them to give him what he deserved, to hurt him, to make sure he never came back, but as I glanced back at Rosie, I knew I was needed here. I needed to be her anchor in that moment, just as she was mine, keeping me on the right path and not drifting back to how I had been in a world before Rosie.

Mike: We just caught him. Rich is taking him back to the mainland.
Pulled him up on some bullshit driving offence. I think he got the hint.

Trent: We also made sure he understood why not to return.

I smirked at the phone, knowing what they'd probably done to convince him not to return. With the tension easing, I walked across the room to hold my girl in my arms.

CHAPTER 11

A Fresh Start

Rosie

Slipping out of Ben's grasp, I gently lowered his tattooed arm back down onto the sofa. The sun had risen but was hidden behind a row of grey clouds, casting a dull light. Tiptoeing across the room, I wrapped my coat back around me as I lifted my bag onto my shoulder. Jason had found me. He knew where I was, I had to leave.

Ben slept peacefully on the sofa, one arm rested behind him and the other curled back round a cushion I had wedged where I once lay. My eyes started to fill with tears at the idea of him waking up and me not being there. We had only known each other a brief time, but he made me feel safe. He made me feel normal. But I wasn't normal—my life had been over before it had really started. My head was gone and I knew I had to leave before Ben could try to stop me.

I picked up my trainers and crept towards the door of Robbie's apartment. One hand on the handle, I twisted when the door came swinging open.

Robbie. I stared up at him before my eyes darted round to a still-sleeping Ben on the sofa. Robbie stared back down at me, taking in my bag on my shoulder. "Going somewhere, princess?" he whispered, both of us glancing round at Ben again, both fearful of what he would do if he caught us in this moment.

Robbie raised his hand to stop me as I tried to make up some excuse. He carried three takeaway coffee cups in his hands. "I can't let you leave, it's stupid. Plus, he'll kill me." Robbie motioned back to Ben.

"Robbie, you have to let me go, it's not safe for me to be here. I'm sorry." Desperation leaked into my voice. "Please!" I half whispered, half pleaded through clenched teeth, tears now escaping from my eyes. His face softened and I took this moment as an opportunity to dart round him and sprint down the stairwell.

"Rosie, stop!" Robbie shouted. Knowing this would wake Ben, I ran faster, still carrying my shoes, stumbling on the stairs.

"Rosie, what the fuck!" It was Ben.

"Shit," I gasped as I missed the last three steps, fell onto my side. I scrabbled to stand up as I heard two sets of footsteps chasing down the stairs behind me. I lifted myself up to hit the exit button to the apartment block, slamming it hard, my trainers still in my hands, and I pushed myself through the heavy door. My eyes darted around, searching desperately for anything I could drive away or anyone who could take me away from here. Realising there was no escape, I sank to my knees, defeated, on the pavement in front of me and let out an ear-splitting scream into the empty road. My belongings fell to my side as I leant my head forward onto the concrete, hands grabbing and pulling at my own hair.

Strong hands reached around my shoulders and lifted me up. Hysterically crying, I allowed myself to be lifted and steered back round towards the apartment block. Robbie watched on with wide eyes as he opened the door for Ben.

When we stopped at the bottom of the stairs, my legs felt like jelly. I was completely paralysed by fear. This feeling of helplessness had broken me again. I couldn't go back there. They wouldn't let me leave and Jason would come back and get me.

Ben twisted me back round to look at him, Robbie watching us. Ben was still only in his boxers, kneeling in front of me—he clearly hadn't had any time to get changed before he'd realised I was leaving.

"Please just let me go," I begged, my voice already showing signs of defeat, barely audible. I couldn't look at them, I didn't want them to see me like this.

Ben shook his head at me before standing up as he pulled me closer to his undressed body. He lifted my arms up around his waist. They dropped down to rest at the sides of my body. Not giving in, Ben lifted me slightly and twisted my legs so he was cradling me as he started to walk back up the stairs. He climbed the stairs easily and waited for Robbie to push open the door. He sat me on the sofa, then pulled on his clothes, sitting down opposite me. Robbie pulled up a chair and sat facing me also. They looked at me as if I was a bomb about to explode.

"You two friends now?" I spat venomously at them, unable to cope with the silence any longer.

They looked at each other, then stared back at me. "We've always been friends, princess," Robbie said tentatively, waiting for my reaction.

"Do you have to keep calling her 'princess'?" Ben groaned, shaking his head at Robbie. I looked at them both sat next to each other. They both had the same dark eyes and soft features. They were both tall and shared the same concerned expression.

Realising I was looking at them together, staring back and forth between the two of them, they had a quick glance at each other then looked back at me, sharing the same mischievous smiles.

"Robbie's my brother," Ben replied, answering my unspoken question.

Of course they were brothers. Everyone on this stupid island knew each other, of course two of my favourite people had to be related. Pretending not to be bothered, I shrugged my shoulders and stared back into their concerned eyes. "So, you're just not going to let me leave then? You'll keep me here …?"

"You're not going anywhere," Ben said with finality.

"You're no different to him then, are you?" I snapped at him, instantly regretting the comparison. Ben let out a callous laugh and stood up slowly, extending himself to his full height as he loomed over me. I stared down at my hands.

"Don't ever compare me to him again," Ben ordered. I nodded without looking back at him. *Too far, Rosie.*

Clearing his throat, Robbie stood up with his brother and walked around to sit next to me. "You're not being held prisoner, princess; we just need to make sure he's gone. You can stay here as long as you need. It's not all bad, I have Netflix and beer and good snacks."

I smiled politely back at him. Maybe it wouldn't be too awful. Ben was still standing, glaring down at me. Unable to avoid him any longer, I slowly turned my head to look at him. He was staring intently back at me. Our eye contact felt like it lasted forever. Taking the hint to leave, Robbie stood up, stretched and headed back over to the kitchen. I continued to stare up at Ben. He looked so disappointed in me.

"Ben …" I desperately hoped he would accept my apology and hear me out. I had to make him understand. He just shook his head at me. "Please, I can't do this, this isn't right, why aren't you letting me go? He knows where I am now, don't you want me to be safe?" I started to stand as I pleaded with him, reaching out and grabbing his hands, shaking them slightly, desperate for him to listen.

"Rosie, *all* I want is for you to be safe. The boys made him leave the island last night. He's not coming back. This is the only way we can keep you safe. They spoke to Gavin, they have Jason's details. Jason won't be able to come back here, that's the only way onto the island. It's sorted, now stop being a brat."

My body relaxed. "So I don't have to stay here with Robbie?" Relief was evident on my face.

He smiled back down at me. "No, you definitely don't have to. But you are going to move in with me. I need to know you're safe."

"Move in? Why would I move in with you? I barely know you. We haven't even … I mean we haven't even seen each other, um, we haven't …"

"Haven't had sex?" Ben asked, his eyebrow arched, amused at my awkward demeanour.

I shrugged back at him. We hadn't. We'd barely spent any time just us two.

"If that's what it will take for you to move in, that can easily be resolved." Ben grinned, winking at me.

"Not on my sofa, it fucking won't." A voice came from the kitchen.

We both laughed, still staring at each other. The tension broke between us as Ben held my hands gently in his. "As for not knowing each other, I agree. I want to take you out, get to know you, learn everything about you. But I have to know you're safe. We can learn all about one another at mine, and if you don't like it, you can always go back to your brother's. Come on, Rosie, just say yes." His dark eyes were full of hope as he waited for my answer.

"Yes," I mumbled, not able to hold eye contact with him.

"What did you say?" he asked again.

"Yes," I replied, raising my voice, still unable to look directly at him.

He lifted my chin with his finger and pulled me in closer for a kiss.

"What did I say about keeping it PG at mine?" Robbie laughed as he walked back in on us, ruining our moment. I pulled away from Ben and walked over to Robbie, wrapping my arms round his waist. He looked down at me, surprised, but pulled me in tightly and rested his cheek on top of my head.

"Thank you, Robbie. Sorry about everything."

"Don't be silly, princess, I'm here for you. Even if it's when my big brother pisses you off, I'll always be here, Rosie." Pulling apart, Robbie looked around the room. "Well, I did get you both coffee, but thanks to Houdini over here it's cold." He nodded his head towards me, smirking as my cheeks reddened.

"It's fine, I'm not thirsty anyway," I said, feeling embarrassed for my failed escape attempt. "Can I go now?"

Ben stared back at me, completely dumbfounded as his head shook in disbelief. "Have you not heard everything that has been said this morning?"

Quickly realising what he thought I meant, I interrupted him. "I'm not trying to leave, I just want to go shopping."

"Shopping? For what?"

"For clothes and stuff. If I'm going to stay, I need some stuff, I only brought one bag with me and I'm running out of shampoo." I felt so stupid for talking about materialistic things in this moment, but it was true. I only had one bra, I had a handful of clothes and two pairs of shoes. I needed to feel more permanent.

"I'll take you shopping," he said, smiling down at me and pulling me to stand closer beside him. "Just let me grab my shoes."

I nodded and gathered my belongings. I folded up the blanket I'd slept on last night and piled it neatly on the sofa. "Thanks, Robbie, for letting me stay. Hopefully see you soon." Robbie winked back at me, retreating into the kitchen.

"Let's go," Ben said as he ushered me towards the door. He looked back at his brother and gave him a nod. We walked back down the stairs I'd last run down. I chuckled to myself, thinking that this morning I'd been so hell bent on getting away from here and now I was walking hand in hand with Ben about to go shopping.

We locked eyes and both started laughing. Ahh, it felt so good to laugh.

Our hands stayed linked together like magnets as we strolled through the local shopping centre. "This is cute," I said for the forty-fifth time, picking up a sleeve of a knitted jumper. Ben lifted it up and added it to the pile of clothes in his arms. "Just because I say something's cute doesn't mean I want to buy it."

"There's no point arguing," he replied, so I didn't. I allowed him to fill his arms with clothes, shampoo and even a new lead for Doug.

As we headed towards the checkouts, I attempted again to pull some of my shopping out of his arms so I could pay. He held on to it with a firm grip, not even acknowledging my attempts to prise a dress out of his hands. He stepped forward to the nearest checkout and placed all the items in a pile as the chirpy sales assistant gazed up at him. She was so busy staring at him she didn't realise I was stood there.

Clearing my throat, I raised my eyebrows at her as she looked at me. Noticing he had his arm wrapped around my shoulders, she shook her head, embarrassed, then busied herself with the till.

Ben was staring down at me, trying to suppress a laugh. I rolled my eyes, then faced forwards as the number on the till was getting higher. I reached into my bag to pull out some cash when he pushed my bag back behind me and pulled out his wallet from his pocket.

"That'll be four hundred and twenty-six pounds, ninety-eight pence then please, is that cash or card?" Her voice was shy and she still didn't give us eye contact. Poor girl, should have just let her flirt with him.

We both replied at the same time, so it came out as a mangled version of the two: "Carshdd."

"I'm sorry, I didn't quite catch …" She let out a small chuckle.

"Card," Ben replied with so much authority, she didn't question my protests and lifted the card machine up to meet his card. She was like putty in his hands.

"Well, thank you very much for shopping with us today," she added as she passed Ben the shopping bags.

"Thanks, darling," he said to her and with a wink he walked away. The girl had turned a shade of beetroot, her jaw slightly open as he walked off.

Smirking, I trailed after the attractive man in front of me. "Thank you," I said as I linked my arm through his. I knew there was no point arguing and I was grateful for his generosity.

He leant down as we walked and kissed me. "You're welcome. Thank you for not arguing too much about it," he retorted, a twinkle in his eye.

We pulled up outside an unfamiliar apartment block. We were so deep into our conversation I hadn't realised we hadn't driven towards number twelve. Noticing my confusion, he picked up his keys in answer to my question.

"This is your place?" I asked. He nodded back at me and smiled as he jumped out of his truck and started to pull my shopping out of the back. "Is there any point bringing that out here?" My question was both leading and trying to be practical. No part of me wanted to carry the heavy shopping bags back and forth too many times.

He turned to face me. "Please don't fight me on this, just stay with me."

"But what about my stuff?" I was panicking now, trying to think of a reason to say no, to slow this down, and failing desperately. Knowing I hadn't packed up all my belongings had made it easier for me to agree to move in with Ben—I'd known I would have time to take this at my own pace. I knew that I had just agreed to stay with him, but this all suddenly felt so real.

"It's here already, Simon dropped it round while we're out. He refused to bring Doug back though, I said we'd pick him up tomorrow."

Ben had moved me out without even talking to me. Too tired to argue, I picked up one of the bags and went to turn back towards the entrance. He pulled the bag out of my hand and lifted the other bags out at the same time, clicking a button on his keys. I followed him towards the main door.

"It's one, four, two, three."

I punched the code into the keypad, scowling at him as I held open the door. He smirked at me, then leant down to kiss me softly on my cheek.

Number fourteen was on the top floor. The flat opened out into an open-plan living space with rich oak floors. The kitchen was white gloss with a marble top and black handles. The living room was filled with an unnecessarily giant TV and a large sofa that was begging to be jumped on. The room was filled with a soft rug and to the right was a round dining room table with mismatched wooden chairs.

Ben placed the bags on the kitchen island and headed towards the coffee machine and started busying himself. I walked through the open-plan space and saw two doors off of the hallway. One was open and showed his bathroom, grey tiles on the floor and wall. A large roll-top bath was stood at one side, matching his and her sinks on the other and a toilet in front of the door. It was suspiciously well designed—despite the enormous TV, you'd have no idea this was a bachelor pad. This hadn't been just his home at some point. The thought made me feel uncomfortable.

Pausing, stuck in my own thoughts, I stood staring blankly at a closed door. This had to be the bedroom. My insecurities pushed me to ask the question I was trying to avoid. "How many other girls have stayed here?"

Ben looked up, his dark eyes narrowing. "You can go in. It's the bedroom, our bedroom now," he said. My heart swelled at the mention of 'our', pulling me out of my jealous mindset thinking about who else had lived here before me. His hand skimmed along my lower back, and I turned to face him. "You're the only one, Rosie. I don't bring people here." His tone was so sincere, I had no reason to doubt him.

I hadn't really thought much about Ben's life before I came crashing into it. Encouraged by his smile, I pushed the wooden door open and looked inside the airy room. This was like a house designed by giants. The bed was huge—made sense, he was massive. The bed was filled with crisp white bedding with black piping round the edge and a large grey throw resting over the edge of the bed. The bed was framed by two bedside tables with large lamps. Above the bed was an old map with pins dotted in the various countries. I wondered if these were places he had been.

This was all feeling a bit too sudden. I had no idea about his life. Spinning around, I walked towards the window. It opened up onto a small balcony where one chair was sat with a table and ashtray. He smoked? The window was dressed with two long curtains pulled back at the sides. I turned back round to face the door and noticed another door in the room, I opened it up shyly and found a ridiculously small walk-in wardrobe, filled mainly with his work uniform and boots. I wondered where my things would fit.

He must have followed me into the room, as he was stood behind me with my old bag Simon had dropped here and a load of shopping bags filled with my new clothes. Shifting my pessimistic mindset, I took in a deep breath, focusing on his dark eyes, and for once I didn't just see the handsome, dark, rugged man I normally saw.

I saw a fresh start.

Ben

Her bright green eyes narrowed before a mischievous grin filled her face. Rosie's face softened as she jumped up with her arms round my neck. Dropping the bags, I held her close. I lifted her legs up so they wrapped round my waist and laughed with her as she began pecking my face with kisses, starting at my cheek and then finding my lips. She silenced my laugh by pressing her lips firmly against mine.

My mouth opened, letting her in. Our tongues danced as our lips moved as one. I grabbed at her behind, pulling her closer. She released my neck as she leaned back slightly. Still holding her upright, I watched as she stripped off her jumper and her T-shirt, then returned her arms back round my neck in an attempt to tug my T-shirt up over my head.

I spun her round and leaned her down onto the bed. I kissed her lips, then trailed kisses down her warm body, careful not to kiss over the scars and avoiding her neck. When I lifted myself up and held my weight above her, Rosie pulled again at my T-shirt, freeing it from my body as I lifted one arm at a time, not losing eye contact with the beautiful girl beneath me. Not hesitating, and driven by the tight strain in my jeans, I pulled at her trousers, opening them up and allowing her to lift herself up so I could pull them down underneath her and throw them out to the side of the bed.

I looked down at her in front of me. Fucking hell. She still looked like she needed to eat more, but the curves of her body excited something inside of me. I stood up quickly and pulled my jeans and my boxers off as one. She looked at me with a wild look in her eyes and slipped her own underwear off as she lay back down, only in her bra.

"Take it off," I demanded between heavy breaths as I stood above her. She stared back at me, her mouth slightly parted, her breathing becoming increasingly shallow.

She unclipped the bra from behind her back, then threw it down at my feet. I leant down and grabbed her from the bed, pulling her up again so she was wrapped round my body, holding her legs up around my waist. I walked her back towards the wall of my bedroom, her back flush against the wall. I lifted her up high so I was able to take one of her nipples into my mouth, my hand on the other as my body pressed her against the wall. She let out a small moan as my tongue teased her. She held on to the back of my head and pushed her breasts further into my mouth. I could hear the excitement build as my tongue circled her nipples and I bit down gently.

I reached down so I could feel between us—she was so ready for me. I teased her gently with one hand as my other hand pulled her hair, bringing her lips up to mine. I swallowed her gasps as I quickened my movements, finding her most sensitive part. She let out a small moan as her legs tightened around me. Fuck, she was ready.

I lifted her back down onto the bed and lowered myself into her. She made a small 'O' with her mouth as I eased myself inside her, entering slowly, careful not to hurt her. Once I was in, eyes glinting as she smiled. I pushed myself into her further, lifting myself up and repeating this again. I reached down and lifted her thighs up either side of me, allowing me to get deeper. She felt so fucking good.

Losing myself inside her, I let out a groan, unable to hold it any more. "Baby, I can't hold it, you feel so—"

"Do it," she managed breathlessly.

"Together, baby," I begged as I reached down and teased her as I entered her again, quickening my pace. I couldn't hold it much longer. I leant down, kissing her forcibly, biting down on her lip as I pulled away. We both tightened around each other as one, our bodies shaking and moans leaving our lips as our mouths, still close, panted against each other. I could feel her convulsing around me as she also found her release.

I looked down at her and smiled. She looked so fucking gorgeous, her smile wide and contagious, her skin shining and that sex hair making a halo around her head on the pillow.

"You look beautiful," I said, leaning down, still inside her. She rolled her eyes and wriggled uncomfortably as I lifted myself out and headed back towards the bathroom.

I came back out and she was sat on the edge of the bed, still completely naked.

"You're going to have to get changed or I'll want to go again," I said, narrowing my eyes at her. She had no idea how irresistible she was.

She let out a glorious laugh and walked past me into the bathroom, brushing her body against mine. Her hand lingered over my muscles.

Fuck, she was so sexy when she was confident and carefree. Checking my watch and realising I was on lates, I changed quickly into my uniform. Rosie came back out with a wide grin lighting up her face to find me fully dressed and perched on the end of the bed.

"Oh, wow, round two? And role play?" she teased.

I threw my T-shirt that I had worn earlier back at her. "Please put something on, I have to go to work and seeing you like that I won't be able to leave."

She pulled the T-shirt on over her head and climbed into my lap. "Then don't leave," she said quietly, looking up at me. I wrapped my arms around her tiny frame as she sat nestled in my lap, trying to take my mind off the fact that she wasn't wearing any underwear below my T-shirt.

"I have to, sweetheart. Relax here, have a bath, watch some TV," I suggested, trying desperately to think of something that came close to comparing to what we had just done.

She let out a cute sigh and folded her arms. She was so adorable I could only laugh down at her and squeeze her tightly against me. "I'm sure I'll find something to entertain myself with. What time will you be back?"

"Earliest I'll be back is ten. Don't wait up for me. I'll be here when you wake up." I really didn't want to leave her, I wanted to spend our first night here together … I wanted to give her a reason to stay.

"Okay, well … stay safe, save lives and all that jazz," she offered as she stood up from my lap, wrapping her arms back around herself.

"Lock the door behind me."

She rolled her eyes at me, leant up and kissed me on the lips.

Standing outside the door, pulling it closed behind me, I waited until I heard the click of the lock before I regretfully headed back down the stairs and away from her. What was wrong with me? I missed her already.

Rosie

I occupied my afternoon with a luxurious bath, filled with bubbles and the fancy shampoo he had bought me. I then spent the rest of the day wrapped in his towel robe, ordering pizza and watching Netflix. I lost myself for a few hours in a book I downloaded on my Kindle until, after one particularly smutty scene, I looked up at the clock on the wall. Eleven-fifteen. He was late. I ignored any intrusive thoughts and wrapped myself up in a blanket on the squishy sofa.

I must have fallen asleep, as I woke up what felt like seconds later by being lifted into strong arms.

"Hey," he whispered into my ear.

Nestling my head into his chest, I smelt an overwhelming smell of smoke and pushed my body away from his in reaction. He lowered me back down. His hair was filled with dust, or ash? His face and arms were covered in black smudges and the smell of burning was so powerful I had to take another step away.

"Sorry, I'll go wash. I didn't want you sleeping on the sofa. Go get into bed and I'll be there in a bit."

I wiped my hands across my eyes and stifled a yawn. "What time is it?" I squinted at the clock—three-thirty in the morning. "Shit, it's really late, you're really late. Are you okay? Is everyone okay? What happened?" The words spilled out of me as panic filled me and my body started to shake.

He stepped towards me, but I mirrored him, stepping back, unable to cope with the overwhelming smell of smoke. Frustrated, he ran his hands through his hair and turned towards the bathroom.

"I'm fine, it's just work, Rosie." He groaned, a hint of annoyance in his voice. I ignored it—he was obviously tired and upset that I wouldn't let him hold me. Choosing to give him some space, I walked over to the plush bed, climbed in and buried my head between the pillows. I fought hard to stay awake, desperately wanting to ask about his night. My heavy eyelids won as I drifted off to sleep.

CHAPTER 12

Mojitos and Taking Control

Rosie

The smell of fresh cooking drifted into the bedroom. When I sat up, still disoriented, my eyes travelled around the room. Remembering where I was, I picked up Ben's soft T-shirt I had worn the night before and pulled it over my head. Rooting through my bag, I picked out clean underwear and a pair of fluffy socks. I glanced at myself in the reflection of the bathroom as I walked past—my hair was wild, I had made a mistake letting it dry naturally.

Following the heavenly smell, I found myself in the kitchen, where I saw my man in front of the hob wearing a navy fire station sweatshirt and his boxer shorts. *My man? Hmm, that's new, kinda like it.* Wrapping my arms around his waist, I smiled up at him. He reached for my face and kissed me.

Holding my breath, I realised I hadn't brushed my teeth. Surely it was too soon for morning breath. I hadn't been with anyone but Jason in such a long time, this was all so new to me.

"Sit down, I'm making breakfast for my girl." He smiled to himself, ignoring my morning breath, and gestured towards the barstools. This felt really fucking domestic.

We sat side by side, tucking into poached eggs and avocado on toast. I managed one egg and half of my avocado toast. Ben looked at my plate, clearly thinking about pushing me to have more. I shook my head slightly, pleading with him to not make me eat any more. My appetite was starting to get better, but I still wasn't there.

My phone beeped and we both looked towards it. He lifted it up towards me as I opened the messages.

> Unknown: Hi Rosie, it's Miranda. I got your number from Robbie. I wanted to know if you fancied a girly night out tonight at the pub. Cocktails?? xx

My brow furrowed as I looked down at the message. Ben rested his elbows on the breakfast bar, staring intently at me.

"What's going through your mind, sweetheart?" He reached across, using his thumb to free my bottom lip I had been chewing on.

"I don't know. How she would have gotten my number. What if it's him?"

Ben shrugged back at me. "Call her back?"

"Will that make me look a bit desperate?" I hadn't had many female friends; I was anxiously hoping this was Miranda.

"Don't overthink it." He reached over to the phone and pressed the little green icon, which set the phone to dial, taking the decision from me.

"Hey." Miranda's sunny voice rang through the phone.

Sighing in relief, I pulled the phone up to my ear. "Hey, girl, sorry, I thought I'd call you back as I'm just"—as I looked round the room, my eyes landed on the radiator—"bleeding the radiator with Ben." Ben's eyes shot up and his huge hand covered his mouth, stifling a laugh that was ready to erupt.

"Weird, but whatever floats both your boats! Did you fancy cocktails tonight then? I'm eager for girl chat."

"Yeah, me too, shall we say seven?"

"It's a date, see ya."

Unable to contain my smile, I beamed at Ben, halting at his worried expression. "What's up, was it the radiator thing?"

"Nothing, it's good for you to have a girlfriend, but do you have to go tonight? I'm working so won't be able to pick you up if I'm late," he added, sounding as if he was sulking slightly.

I laughed at him. "I'll be fine. Please, I want to go. I don't want to sit here and wait for you to come home again."

He smiled and squeezed my leg slightly. I returned to my phone, saving her number and shooting her a message.

Me: Can't wait for some mojitos! xo

"You're not going to drink too much, are you?" he asked, cringing slightly as he read the message about the mojitos.

"I can't promise anything." I laughed, leaning over to kiss him. He grabbed me by my waist, lifted me up and carried me to the bedroom. I guessed I could get used to living here.

Ben changed into his swoon-worthy uniform as I watched, still completely naked and sated inside his warm bed. After he left for work, I decided to spend time reading, unpacking and choosing what to wear tonight. After trying on everything I owned, I settled on a pair of black skinny jeans and a burgundy red wrap-around top with capped sleeves.

Slipping on my black chunky heels, I spent the next hour trying to control and straighten my wild dark hair. I finished off with a small bit of makeup and picked up my bag.

The Swan was a convenient ten-minute walk from Ben's building. Already regretting not bringing a coat, I headed into the warm, welcoming entrance of the pub. Miranda was sat at one of the raised tables by the bar, a mojito in front of her and a spare one by the empty seat.

I rushed over and greeted Miranda with a warm, appreciative smile. She was a beauty; her long golden hair was styled up in a high pony tail and she was wearing a little black dress with long sleeves and chunky heels that matched mine.

We spent the next four hours chatting, laughing, gossiping and drinking mojitos. We ignored the men who attempted to join us in our bubble and continued with our girls' night. We laughed hard as she shared details about how she was trying to break her and Joey's dry spell. Having a friend made my heart so happy.

Strong arms wrapped around my waist. I started to go into bitch mode, telling the intruder that we weren't interested, when I recognised the familiar smell of smoke and Ben's cologne. He gave me a crooked smile and shrugged—of course he couldn't stay away from girls' night and, by the looks of it, neither could Mike, Trent, and Jim. Ben leant down and whispered in my ear as his hand rested at the back of my neck, his words tickling my neck and sending tingles down my spine. "You look absolutely stunning, baby."

I smiled up at him with drunk eyes and he shook his head affectionately, pulling my back tight against his rock-solid chest. Trent introduced himself to Miranda and headed off to the bar, returning with two more mojitos and four pints of beer.

We spent the rest of the evening laughing together, hearing stories about the boys' misfortunes and embarrassing conquests. My whole body felt warm from the mojitos, but I felt so damn happy in this moment. It felt so good to laugh with friends and not have to worry about the consequences. Not have to worry if I laughed at the wrong joke, if I laughed too loud.

A few more faces joined our table and Ben introduced me to all of them as 'my Rosie.' *Urgh, swoon.*

We had moved to a bigger table, as there were now sixteen of us, but I might have counted people twice—the mojitos had really gone to my head. Joey and Robbie were two familiar faces who had joined. I enthusiastically greeted Robbie by jumping onto him, wrapping my arms and legs round him like a koala as he walked past my table, causing us both to fall to the floor in a heap of giggles. Excitement over, I was now sat in Ben's lap, leaning my head drunkenly against his shoulder, only raising it to reply politely to one of his friends making conversation.

Jim came to sit down beside us, pulling a redhead down next to him.

"Who's your friend?" I slurred at him.

He let out a laugh, reached over and pinched my cheek. "This is Red. Red, meet Rosie." I looked over at the girl as she pouted back at me.

"My name's not Red." She rolled her eyes.

"It is tonight," he replied, pulling her against him and leading her out of the door of the pub. I looked up at Ben and raised my eyebrows.

"Let me take you home, I'm done sharing you," he whispered as he tucked my hair back behind my ear. He stroked his fingers through my hair. "You look so different with your hair like this," he muttered against my ear.

"Good or bad?" I asked, unable to say much more due to the copious amounts of mojito in my system.

"You always look good," he replied tactfully. *Smooth.*

I turned to look at him. "Not when we first met, I looked like shit."

"Yeah, you were still beautiful, but I can't ever see you like that again. This is much better, happy suits you," he added as he continued to play with my hair.

We were interrupted by a drunk Miranda being steered through the crowd by Joey, his hands firmly on her shoulders keeping her upright. She threw herself onto me, pulling me up slightly off of Ben to wrap her arms around me.

"I freaking love you, bitch," she wailed, pulling me tighter.

"I really, really want us to be friends and for you to come round when Ben leaves me alone and works because he's boring," I slurred back, not entirely sure we were making any sense.

"I really want to watch *Grey's Anatomy* with you and drink mojitos," she replied, her eyes rolling back slightly as Joey steadied her. Standing to face her, I just nodded as if I understood what this meant. Joey and Ben shared a look and hid their amusement as our emotional goodbye continued. We stood there for a while, being propped up by one another, before they gently separated us and Joey steered her back out of the pub. Leaning back, I glanced up at Ben, who could no longer contain his laughter.

"Shut up, I like her, she's a bad bitch."

He patted my shoulder, soothing me. "She is indeed. Come on, let me take you home."

Home. He felt like home, but I was way too drunk to tell him.

We made our goodbyes, which took forever as I insisted on saying goodbye to everyone in the pub, not just those in our group. Trent lifted me up and carried me over his shoulder whilst Ben was distracted saying goodbye to Robbie and some other friends. I was paraded around the pub and carried back to Ben. He snatched me back from Trent and used one hand to push Trent's shoulder away from me, detaching us completely.

"Bye, Trenty," I managed as a slightly-pissed-off Ben carried me back out of the pub. Trent laughed, then quickly got distracted by a blonde who walked past.

Ben

She fell asleep on the way home, her face pressed up against the door, which made it almost impossible for me to get her out of the car without waking her. I pulled the door open and her head flopped down towards the pavement. Somehow, I scooped my arms under the door quickly enough to catch her before she fell. I lifted her up so I could carry her over my shoulder up the steep stairs, a fireman's lift.

Laying Rosie down on the bed, I brushed her hair out of her face and began to remove her shoes when she stood up quickly and bolted towards the bathroom. She took a dive and landed in front of the toilet, where with one loud retch she brought up all of the mojitos she had drunk. Her hands were steadying herself either side of the toilet and her whole body was shaking. I knelt down beside her and held her hair back in one hand and rubbed her back with the other. She clearly couldn't handle her alcohol; annoyance flooded my mind.

Sitting back against the cold bath, I was still holding her hair with one hand as she continued to throw up. Noticing her bag was still wrapped round her, I lifted up the strap clumsily around her head. Her phone, purse and cigarettes fell out—didn't know she smoked, maybe it was a drinking thing. Her phone was flashing and I couldn't help my curiosity. I looked at her lock screen, where I could see a preview of a message.

Unknown: You looked good tonight, babe, although you know I don't like your hair like that.

And below, the same unknown had sent through an image. I picked the phone up and held it close to my face. From the tiny preview, it looked like it was taken from inside the pub.

My heart started to beat against my chest. Who was telling my girl how to wear her hair? Who the fuck was taking pictures of her? I looked down at Rosie, who had now fallen back asleep, her head resting on the seat of the toilet. I put her phone into my back pocket and lifted her up off of the floor and back towards our bedroom. I removed her clothes and placed her underneath the comforter, tucking her in so she lay on her side, tactfully placing a washing-up bowl underneath her.

Still thinking about those text messages, I started pacing the hallway. I looked down at my phone and checked the time. Two-ten in the morning, too late to do anything right now, but I had to know who this was and what they wanted. The worst-case scenario filled my mind. Unable to think of anything else, I sat waiting on the sofa till the clock got to six. I lifted my phone up and sent a message:

Me: Hi mate, I really need a favour. Can you please come by mine today? I'll make sure I'm in all day.

Rich: Is she finally ready to press charges? I still have all the photos from the hospital, I just need her statement and for her to meet with one of the domestic violence advocates.

Me: She hasn't agreed yet, but she needs to. I think he's back.

Rich: I'll come by with a colleague later, make it official. You'll have a
few hours to convince her.

Me: Cheers, mate, I owe you.

I needed to wake her up—she would understand once I explained
why. I had been awake for so long, I couldn't wait any longer.

I sat on the side of the bed and shook her shoulders, not being as
gentle as I usually would. She turned round and looked at me, scowling.
"What the fuck? Fuck off, you fucking fuck!"

"Don't swear at me, and I'm sorry. Get up, please, we need to talk," I
said, easing her up to a sitting position.

"Whoa, stop. What's wrong?" she asked, sitting back up against the
headboard of the bed. She looked tiny against it, and I suddenly felt a
pang of guilt for waking her up that way. "What are you doing with my
phone?" she asked, slightly annoyed as I joined her so both our backs
were resting against the headrest, our feet stretched out in front of us.
"You're scaring me. Why are you on my phone?"

"I don't want to scare you, I'm sorry," I said, reaching out and
squeezing her hand. "Last night, I saw you had some messages, and I need
you to unlock your phone and tell me whom they're from. I can guess, but
I need to know."

She looked at me, a puzzled and annoyed expression across her face.
"I haven't done anything wrong," she retorted defensively.

My breathing wavered as I realised what this looked like. "I know,
Rosie, I'm not checking up on you, I promise. I wouldn't do that. Here,
look."

She picked up her phone and opened the messages from 'unknown'. I
looked over her shoulder as she read, now able to read the full text.

Unknown: You looked good tonight, babe, although you know I don't like your hair like that. Aren't you missing someone to tell you exactly how to do your hair and how to wear your clothes so you don't send out the wrong message? I've been watching you, babe, you're not behaving yourself, you're embarrassing yourself ... everyone can see right through you, you're damaged goods, babe, and I'm the only one who will ever accept you for what you are. It's embarrassing seeing you all over men, letting them carry you around and parade you around. You're a pathetic cunt and you need to come back home. I'll wait till you're ready. The longer I wait, the worse it will be when we're back home.

Unknown: *images*

The image showed Rosie hanging over Trent's shoulder, being carried through the pub. The next picture was of Rosie, by herself, walking from my apartment to the Swan. The last image had been taken outside of this apartment, me carrying Rosie through the entrance. He'd been here.

I was shaking. I couldn't see straight. I could only think about what I'd do to him. Rosie was starting to look green again. Her eyes were unfocused and her expression vacant. She pulled her knees up to her chest and, releasing my hand, she wrapped her arms around her legs and started to rock.

"This is it, Rosie, you're talking to the police today. I don't want to hear anything else out of your mouth other than 'okay'. Do you understand? You need to take control." I hated myself for speaking to her like this, but I didn't know how else to make her hear how serious this was.

"Okay," she said, not looking at me, just complying.

That had been too easy. She was too amenable, but I couldn't have it both ways. I turned around and walked towards the door, not able to see her like this.

"You know this is going to end up with him killing me if you make me do this?" she said, barely audible and still not looking at me.

"It won't, because I will kill him before he ever gets the chance to come anywhere near you again. I'm not a good guy, Rosie. I can't control myself when it comes to protecting those I care about. I won't lose you; I won't lose anyone again because I was unable to protect them."

Strolling over to the balcony, I pulled the door open and sat in the one seat. Closing the door with one arm, I reached under the chair and grabbed the old box of cigarettes, putting one to my mouth and lighting it. I inhaled deeply, allowing the smoke to hit the back of my throat and leaning my head back, willing the tension to release.

The door to the balcony opened again and Rosie stepped out, now covered in my dressing gown and walking towards me. She sat down in between my legs and lifted her legs so they balanced her against me and the railing of the balcony. She reached into the dressing gown and pulled out a cigarette. She turned round to face me, cupping her hands around the cigarette. I lit it for her. She turned back, leant against me, took her first drag and let out a huge exhale.

"You going to tell me what you meant? Who did you lose, Ben?" she asked tentatively.

I chose to ignore her. "Rich will be round soon. Please just talk to him and don't fight me on this. I want to keep you safe, but you have to keep yourself safe. You can't coast through life not taking any actions. Nothing will change. Take. Control. Rosie."

She stayed still for a moment, then nodded, stubbing out her cigarette and lifting herself from my lap to head back inside. She wasn't happy, but

I didn't care. I rubbed the scar on my face, a constant reminder of what I'd lost. There wasn't a chance I would risk losing her too.

Two hours later, I was sat in the bedroom alone. Rich had arrived with another police officer named Greg and the domestic violence advocate, Emma. Rosie wouldn't let me listen to the interview or the assessment. I didn't argue. I sat in the bedroom, my legs shaking and my mind racing. After they all left, Rosie came to see me in the bedroom and dropped an envelope in front of me.

"This sums it up," she muttered, still not giving me eye contact and heading back towards the living room. I heard the TV power up and the sound of the sofa as she sat back down.

I emptied the contents of the envelope to the side of me, onto the grey throw. Out came six photos, injuries I recognised from when we'd found Rosie. I glanced at them quickly, my stomach dropping as I tried not to imagine what had happened to her. One picture showed the inside of her thighs covered in dark bruises and scratch marks. I felt sick. I picked up the sheet of paper inside of the envelope: 'Domestic Abuse Risk Assessment.' Recognising Rosie's scribbles, I started to read:

1. Has it resulted in injury? Yes
2. Are you frightened? Yes
4. Do you feel isolated from family/friends? Yes
5. Are you feeling depressed or having suicidal thoughts? Yes
6. Have you separated or tried to separate within the past year? Yes
7. Is there conflict over child contact? No
8. Do they control everything you do? Yes
9. Have they ever used weapons or objects to hurt you? Yes
10. Have they ever threatened to kill you and you believed them? Yes
11. Have they ever attempted to strangle/choke/suffocate/drown you? Yes

12. How long were you with them? 5 years

13. Have they ever been in trouble with the police or have any police history? No

14. Have you ever sought help before? Yes

15. Any other relevant information? (Do they have access to weapons, e.g., military, police etc.) Yes—they're a police officer

The last answer caught my attention. I stared blankly at the paper in my now-shaking hands. I didn't know what to say. I'd known it was bad, but I hadn't known it was this bad. My eyes fell on the last answer. I understood now why she was so scared, how he had managed to influence those idiot coppers to interview her. I didn't know what to do in that moment. All I wanted to do was hold her and comfort her, but I could tell she needed space. I stood up, paced around the room, then decided we needed a distraction.

I walked back into the living room, stood facing Rosie and reached out to her. She looked at me blankly and turned back round to face the TV. I grabbed her arm and pulled her upright. "If you could do anything today, what would it be? Anything in the world."

She shook her head and looked down at her feet. I tilted her head back so she was looking up at me. Reaching down, I wrapped her arms around my neck and lifted her underneath the back of her thighs so her legs wrapped round my waist.

"Not this," she said, sulking still.

I laughed and squeezed her behind. "I know, beautiful, but seriously, anything."

"I just want to stay in, chill, watch TV and eat doughnuts. I'm so hungover and you made me do that this morning." She blinked fast, her eyes brimming with tears. She was exhausted.

"Okay, fine, sit back down. We'll watch whatever you want and I'll get someone to drop us off some doughnuts," I said, trying to pacify her. She sat back down onto the sofa, tucking her legs underneath her and huddling under a blanket.

Thinking quickly, I called Simon. "Hi, mate, just wondering if you fancied coming over. Rosie is really hungover, plus she had to speak to the police this morning. She did great. She's just sad and I think she'd like to see you guys."

"Say no more, I'll bring the doughnuts," he replied before he ended the call.

We were ten minutes into an old *Dinner Date* episode when Simon, Archie and Louis all came through the door, Louis holding three boxes of doughnuts. Rosie's eyes lit up at the sight of her brothers and the doughnuts—mainly the doughnuts. Simon had a squirming Doug under his arms.

Doug ran back over to his mum and showered her in puppy kisses. Louis sat down next to his sister, placing the doughnuts on the coffee table. He put his arm around her and pulled her back into his side and away from me. She wrapped her arm across his stomach and buried her head in his chest. He kissed her on top of the head and started rubbing her arm, both siblings seeking comfort from each other in complete silence.

We all spent the rest of the afternoon eating doughnuts, laughing and watching crap TV. I looked over at Rosie; she was asleep in her brother's arms. I wanted to be the one to give her comfort and peace. Why was I feeling jealous of her brother? My phone beeped, distracting me from my thoughts.

Rich: It's taken care of for now. He's been cautioned, we've taken him into custody. The restraining order is in place. I'll let you know if we need anything more.

Me: Thank you, I owe you so much.

Rich: Nah, I enjoyed arresting him today. I've never seen anything like those photos, and what she told us, she didn't deserve any of that.

Purposefully ignoring what he meant by 'what she told him', I looked over at Rosie, still sleeping and now gently snoring against Louis. I reached down and lifted her up, breaking their contact.

Louis stood up at the same time. "Let's go." He motioned for Archie and Simon to follow him.

"No, please stay, wait for me to come back. I need to talk to you all," I said as I walked away, holding Rosie close. I placed her in the big bed, tucking her in under the comforter, brushing her curls away from her peaceful face. I came back to the three men sat awkwardly in my living room as I sat back down in my seat.

"Thanks for staying, I just wanted to update you on what's been happening," I said, clearing my throat and getting ready to tell them everything. They all stared blankly at me after I filled them in on what had been going on. Archie nodded, but didn't stop—he continued nodding his head and looking from his husband to his brother, waiting for someone else to talk. Louis gave one nod back at his brother, then shook his head, motioning for him to stop.

"Thanks, Ben, it sounds like she will be safe now, which is all we want too. We're just a bit shocked, I think," Simon stammered out, still staring at his nodding husband. "I think I better take Noddy here home." He stood up, supporting a still-in-shock Archie back through the door.

Louis was still comfortably sat on the sofa, showing no signs of moving. I walked over to the fridge, got two beers. Twisting off the caps, I handed one to Louis and sat down next to him, bringing my beer to my lips. I took a deep swig, then turned towards him.

"Go on, say what you want to say," I said calmly, waiting for the 'older brother talk'.

"I don't actually have anything to say, just know if you hurt her at all, if you so much as make her cry and I hear about it, I will kill you."

"Okay." I didn't plan on hurting her, so agreed to his threat. "What's up with your parents?" I asked the question I had been thinking about for a while. Why was this girl being supported by her brothers and not her parents?

"Mum's dead, she killed herself. Dad's as good as dead, an alcoholic, no use to any of us," Louis said in between swigs.

"I'm sorry. I didn't know," I said, shocked that this hadn't come up before.

"You and Ro don't talk much then, do you? I would have thought she'd have told you about how she found Mum—"

"She found her?" I interrupted. Why hadn't this come up? We hadn't really spoken about our families. I hadn't talked to her about mine, I'd only just admitted that Robbie was my brother.

"Yeah, it was rough. Rosie was so fucking young. Try explaining that to a fourteen-year-old. My dad fell apart, turned to drink, lost his job, lost his house. They all moved in with me and my girlfriend. Was ridiculous, but some of my favourite memories are from inside that flat.

"Rosie's the youngest, it affected her most. She moved out when she was nineteen when she met Jason. We didn't really see her much after that.

We knew something was up, we didn't know anything was physical. I'm the oldest and I have my own family now, so can't come and be with her all the time. I think she's safe with you. I've told my missus Rachel that she's happy with you. Please don't prove me wrong."

I let him carry on. I had never heard him speak so much, I could tell he needed to get it out.

"She wants to visit soon, with the kids. We thought maybe for Rosie's birthday we could all spend some time together."

I looked at him, questioning what he'd last said.

"Her birthday is in two weeks' time." He answered my unspoken question.

I nodded thankfully, feeling ashamed that I probably would have never known this. I guessed if after a year she hadn't had a birthday I'd maybe have thought about it.

CHAPTER 13

The Impact of Trauma

Ben

For fuck's sake, it felt like I had only just drifted off to sleep. Picking up my ringing phone, I glanced first at the time. Six-fifteen.

"Yep," I grunted, still groggy.

"You're going to hate me," Rich said tentatively.

"What?"

"She's going to have to come in. We need to ask a few questions. He's been at the station, filing a complaint against her. I don't think anything will come out of it, mate, but it's—"

I interrupted him. "When?"

"Today. Need her to be here as soon as possible, really, mate."

"I'll bring her by after work."

"Needs to be this morning, it's in her best interest. Trust me."

"Rich … don't do this. I can't, I have to go to work, and she can't do this alone."

"Can't one of her brothers go?" Rich asked.

I let out a deep sigh. "I'll figure it out." And with that I hung up, chucking my phone back onto the bed.

I explained to Rosie what Rich had requested. It seemed like she had expected what was to come. She got changed without another word.

A knock at the door made her flinch—the thought of being back around the police had put her on edge. I walked across the flat and opened the door. Trent stood there with a crooked smile plastered on his face. He put his hand to his head in a mock salute. "Reporting for duty, boss." He stamped his foot, then made himself comfortable on the sofa.

Rosie walked back into the room and sat down beside Trent, perched on the edge of the sofa, her nervous energy radiating from her as she tapped her feet and played with the strap on her bag. Trent pulled her into his side and held her close to him. A pang of jealousy coursed through me, but I let him comfort her. I was grateful we could cover him so he could go with her.

I watched him hold her, feeling useless. She looked so uncomfortable and the small bit of confidence she had gained since coming to the island was gone. She even looked slightly different, her hair pulled up into a messy bun and her eyes glazed over and absent. I knew her well enough by now to know that her eyes glazing over was her version of putting up a wall, the only way she knew how to protect herself, her coping mechanism. It was the sign to show me she was scared. It physically hurt watching her, knowing I couldn't support her today.

We talked about what her ex could have on her. She recalled one night where he had been drinking with his friends and forced himself on top of her in front of them and in her panic she'd picked up the nearest object, which happened to be a screwdriver, which she'd jammed into his thigh as he was on top of her. I tried to stay calm as she told me. I later walked outside just to punch something.

Now Rosie got into Trent's car and I watched as she fumbled with her seat belt, hands shaking. Trent saw this too and gently pulled the belt over her and fastened it.

I leant down and kissed Rosie on the head. "You've got this, sweetheart. Trent's with you. He won't leave you." I looked up at Trent, who nodded once. "And if anything happens he'll call me."

She pursed her lips, looked up at me and gave me a brief second of eye contact before nodding her head and looking forward again. I shut her door and watched helplessly as they drove away.

Rosie

We stayed in silence for the rest of the journey. Trent hummed along to the radio and started talking to me about his fantasy football team. To take a guess, this was more to fill the silence rather than him actually enjoying the songs that played at nine a.m. on a Tuesday or thinking he had any chance of getting me to create my own team.

Trent wrapped his arm around my shoulders as we walked in through reception and announced ourselves to the officer at the desk. She motioned for us to sit on the chairs in the waiting room. Before we got to sit down, Rich had appeared and was looking uneasy.

"Hey, Rosie, sorry about this. Procedures and all," he said as he begrudgingly led me through the double doors. He looked back at Trent, questioning why he was following us.

"I'm not leaving her side, mate."

Rich nodded and led us both towards an interview room. Sitting down, I hesitantly glanced towards the recording device.

"Rosie, you're not under caution, but before I turn that on I would advise you to think very carefully about your answers." He looked around, making sure we were out of earshot. "If, for example, you did anything in self-defence, it's important to use that terminology."

I gave him a weak smile; I trusted him because Ben trusted him. I used the term 'trust' loosely, but I didn't think he was lying.

The recording device beeped. "Can you please confirm your name for the tape?" Rich asked.

"Yes, Rosie Robinson."

"Thank you. For the purpose of the tape I am DS Richard Owens and in the room is Rosie Robinson, and supporting Miss Robinson is Mr Trent Mariano. Miss Robinson—"

"Rosie, please," I squeaked, feeling uncomfortable being addressed as 'Miss Robinson'.

"Okay, Rosie. Please can you confirm you know this man in the picture I'm showing you? For the purpose of the tape, I'm showing Article 23b."

"Yes, I know who he is." I felt instantly sick, that feeling of unease becoming overpowering.

"By name, please, Rosie, and what relation do you have to him?"

I struggled to say his name out loud. I steadied my breath, swallowing down the bile rising from my stomach. Rich smiled at me reassuringly, nodding as Trent eyed the picture, taking it all in. "His name is Jason Mathers and he's my ex-boyfriend," I blurted out, barely pausing between each word.

"Mr Mathers has made an allegation of assault by yourself against him. He reports that you stabbed him."

Here it went. So fucking predictable. Leaving Jason and forming what my therapist would describe as a healthy relationship with Ben had really given me some perspective. When I'd been with Jason, I'd never known his next move, which had left me in a constant state of fear, but taking a step back, I just felt so damn stupid for not realising what he was doing.

"Rosie, did that happen?" Rich stared at me and mouthed the words 'self-defence'.

"Yes, in self-defence," I answered compliantly, my heart racing as I tried not to think about what had happened, silently begging him to not ask me.

"Please can you explain to me what happened?"

Fuck's sake. "Yes, um, he was on top of me and I … I …" I stuttered, putting my hands to my face, trying to focus my mind and stop myself from going back to how it had felt. "He had been drinking and he wanted to have sex with me," I started.

Trent sat forward in his chair, shaking his head.

"He tried to take my clothes off and his friends were there and I said no. I promise I told him no, but he didn't like that and he was laughing and I remember the smell of whisky, it was so strong, he put his hands down on my … my … my vagina and I remember it hurting and I told him no, please, but he didn't stop, I needed it to stop. I had no choice, I picked up whatever I could reach and I pushed it into him. It was a screwdriver, we were in his garage. He stopped trying to sleep with me, but he punched me three times in the face … I think I passed out and I think he had sex with me anyway, I woke up naked on the floor …" My voice trailed off as what I thought was bile continued to rise from my stomach.

"I'm going to be sick," I warned as I lurched forward. Rich tactfully pushed a bin beneath me as Trent leapt forward, his hands resting on my back.

"That's enough now, mate, I think you've got what you need." Trent shook his head. His face was pale.

Rich reached across, turned off the tape and sat in silence as they both watched me continue to be sick. Maybe this was rock bottom. It couldn't get worse than this. Surely.

"I'm really sorry, Rosie."

I nodded quickly before I returned to my vomiting. Heat prickled inside me, making me feel faint. "I don't feel good, it's so hot in here, I feel hot. I feel so fucking hot." I ripped off my jumper. I had a sudden awareness of my clothes touching my skin, feeling tighter and tighter, strangling me. I started to scratch at my arms, I just wanted to get out of my skin. I couldn't articulate it in any way that would make sense to these men in this moment.

Trent looked at me in horror as I stood from my chair, pacing in a small vest top that showed way too much skin. "Doll, sit down. Stop doing … that," he said, unable to find words to describe what I was doing as I paced up and down the small room, my nails digging into my skin as I wrapped my arms tight around myself. I must have looked like I'd escaped from somewhere. I wanted to escape from my skin.

I couldn't look at him. I paced back and forth trying to steady my breathing. I felt Jason's hands back on me, I could almost taste the whisky that had been on his breath that night.

I let out a tortured scream and fell to the floor, trying to block out the images. Curling right down onto my knees, my head pressed against the hard vinyl floor, I covered my ears with my hands. I could still hear the laughs from his friends and feel the pressure of his first punch flying straight into the side of my head.

"Doll, you're scaring me," Trent whispered in my ear, reaching his arm round me, trying to comfort me. I flinched away from him, backing myself into the corner of the room, still sat against the floor.

"What should I do?" Rich asked.

"You shouldn't have asked her those fucking questions!" Trent shouted. "Go get Ben, he's going to fucking kill you," Trent said, a hint of fear in his voice as he sat back down on the floor beside me, not touching me.

I heard the distant dialling tone of Rich's phone. "Hi, Ben, I … yeah, she's here still, but she …"

"Pass it here, you prick!" He lifted the phone to his ear, his dark eyes still on me. "Ben, she's freaking out, she puked, she tried to take off her clothes and I think she's made herself bleed and she's huddled on the floor, and she won't let me touch her." Trent's voice started to break towards the end of his sentence. "Rosie, Ben is on the phone, angel, he wants to speak to you—"

"No." I intercepted him before he had a chance to pass me the phone.

"You hear that?" Trent said into the phone. "Okay, yeah, we'll be here."

Tightening my grip over my ears, trying to block out any feeling, I could feel Jason's hands on me, holding me down and forcing himself into my underwear.

I didn't know how much, but I knew time passed. Rich was still sat in his chair, his head in his hands, and Trent remained sitting beside me on the floor. Ben walked through the door and closed it right behind him. He looked first at Rich, who couldn't give him eye contact, then down towards Trent, who stood up quickly, shaking his head at Ben before taking his seat again.

I felt Ben's strong hands on my forearms, which were holding my knees tight to my chest. "Hey, baby, I'm here, you feel so cold. Where's your …"

Trent passed him my jumper. Ben stretched open the neck and gently guided it onto me. I feebly lifted my arms to help him dress me, my mind elsewhere, unable to focus on this simple task.

Jumper now on, I looked up into his eyes, instantly feeling safe. He was my safe space. I climbed into his arms as he was crouched down in front of me. He effortlessly lifted me into the air and onto my feet. My knees buckled slightly, but he caught me, holding me tight. "You need anything else or can I take my girl home?"

"No. That's it," Rich muttered, unable to look at either of us. Trent followed as Ben led me out of the room and back out into the main reception.

I heard him before I saw him, the tap-tap-taps of his rings against a solid surface that had conditioned me to automatically flinch. When I looked up, piercing blue eyes leered over at me. I stopped, my legs collapsing beneath me. My heart skipped a beat as my eyes locked with the familiar face. A sheet of ice dropped through my body. All the strength Ben had just given me to stand up had vanished.

Jason was stood at the main desk. He looked over at me, yellowing bruises covered the side of his face. Seeing the effect he still had on me, he smirked triumphantly. The sound of his rings against the desk echoed across the sparse space.

My body stopped and I couldn't move despite Ben trying to lead me forward. He looked down at me and traced my eye line back to my ex-boyfriend, who was still stood grinning at the desk.

Ben went to move towards him. I grabbed at his arm, trying to prevent him. Ben stopped, realising I needed him in that moment.

Trent stormed past without either of us being quick enough to react. He swung his arm back and smashed his fist into Jason's smug face. A sharp crack and a splash of blood didn't stop Trent as he swung his arm back again, ready to put all of his anger into his punch as Rich rushed over from behind, grabbing Trent's elbow and swinging him round.

"Enough. Get out of here now!" he demanded, the authority echoing across the reception.

Jason stood up, wiping the blood from his mouth as he looked back over to me and Ben and winked. Ben stiffened and I could tell if I wasn't attached to him, he also would have unleashed hell just as Trent had.

Ben steered me over to my ex, still with his arms guiding and supporting my body. I dug my heels in, unable to get closer, my body physically rejecting any attempts to go near him again.

"You're fucking scum," Ben said. "You'll never come near her again or I will kill you, do you understand me?"

Jason laughed. "She'll come back to me; you'll see."

"She's mine now and she'll never come back to you. You'll. Never. Harm. Her. Again," Ben warned.

"I think there's been some misunderstanding. Rosie likes it rough, don't you, babe? Someone as stupid as Rosie needs a little guidance on life. You like it when I take control, don't you, babe?" He put on a sickly smile.

I couldn't look at him. Something I had learnt in our relationship was to avoid all eye contact. He didn't like it when I stood up to him; he told me it was disrespectful for me to look directly in his eyes. My body was back to submissive mode in his presence.

Jason took a step towards us as Ben reached out his arm as a barrier, protecting me against Jason's advances. It was too much. I wriggled out from under his arm and raced towards the door. Ben turned and followed me as Trent held open the door, staring at my ex, daring him to come forward. I raced towards Ben's truck and stood at the passenger door. As soon as Ben clicked the keys I jumped inside and locked the door behind me. Looking up, I saw Ben speaking with Trent outside their cars. They kept turning to look at me, Ben brushing his hand through his hair.

Ben drove me home and walked me up to the flat. I reached into my suitcase, which still wasn't fully unpacked, and grabbed a packet of sleeping tablets I had brought with me.

"What are those?" Ben asked, clearly concerned as he stood over me. I looked back up at him, swallowed two dry without answering him, then climbed into bed. My body and mind needed me to sleep. I needed to not think about that night. I needed something to drown out the sounds of their laughs.

Ben

Cautiously, I watched as she climbed up into our bed and I looked down at the packaging of the tablets she had just taken. She hadn't needed to take these since she had been with me. She needed to rest. I climbed on top of the comforter and hugged her into me. She flinched, but I held her close. I wouldn't let go. She was a wreck, she wasn't acting like the survivor I knew she was. One glimpse of him and she was back to how she'd been when she'd been with him.

"Ben," her small voice chirped beneath the comforter.

"Yes, sweetheart?"

"When I wake up, I don't want to talk about today."

"I know."

"I don't want to see him again either."

"You won't."

"I don't want to see Rich either."

"Okay." My mind started swimming. He had pushed her too far.

"I'm not talking to any more police officers," she added.

"We'll talk about it later."

"We'll talk about it never."

"Rosie, if you don't, I won't be able to protect you here, so that will mean sending you off to live with my mum or something and you don't want that, so go to sleep and drop it."

"I didn't know you had a mum."

"For the best. She's evil, a lousy cook and you wouldn't want to live with her, so go to sleep."

She rolled over, tucking her face against me. I waited until I could hear her familiar soft snores before I shut my eyes and allowed myself to rest with her.

CHAPTER 14

An Incredibly Happy Birthday

Rosie

We had slipped into a routine. Ben would go to work, I would busy myself around the flat, walking Doug and meeting up with my new friend Miranda. We hadn't discussed me getting a job again and I was starting to finally enjoy not being a slave for the National Health Service. I didn't miss night shifts; I didn't miss the constant sadness and stress each shift brought.

I spent a lot of time reading. I downloaded book after book on my Kindle and spent time reading in the bath, while at the park walking Doug, or even as I traipsed round the supermarket doing the shopping. I lost myself in different worlds, the perfect distraction to keep my mind positive and focused on feeling better.

It was getting closer to my birthday. I hadn't celebrated my birthday in a long time, not properly, since before my mum passed away. My brothers tried to always make it fun for me with pizza, ice cream and their attempts at buying a young girl birthday presents, which usually resulted in a toy tool kit or a Nerf gun. Jason didn't think it was anything to celebrate. I wondered if this year would be any different. Suddenly realising I was being stupid, I stood up and busied myself with the rest of the washing-up. Of course it wouldn't be any different. How would Ben know it was my birthday?

We had made a conscious effort to get to know each other more over the past couple of weeks, playing endless games of twenty questions. He would interrupt me as I was in the bath, walking in to ask me my favourite country I'd been to or my favourite football team. Those questions were easy; I had only been to Paris outside of the UK and I despised football.

I'd been sitting on the toilet, toilet paper in hand, the last time Ben had barged in.

"Who did you vote for at the last general election?" he said, panic in his eyes. Noticing I was sat on the toilet, he jumped and turned to head back through the door and hit his face against the door frame. Chaos erupted. He swore and staggered round the bathroom as I half shouted at him to get out and half burst into hysterical laughter at the madness in front of me. Doug was barking loud beneath his feet, panicking that he was trying to attack his mum.

"Get out, you nutter!" I shouted, throwing the roll of paper at Ben's head as he staggered blindly out of the door, into the hallway.

I flushed the toilet and washed my hands, returning to the kitchen, where he sat at the breakfast bar with frozen peas held against his eyes. I walked up towards him and stroked my hand down the side of his face, kissing him on the forehead. "You're very sweet with this whole 'getting to know me' thing. Plus that will live forever in my mind rent-free." I tried to hide my amusement.

He dropped the peas and held me close. "I just want to know everything about you," he said, a hint of sadness in his voice.

"You will. We've got our whole lives to learn about each other." That slipped out way too easily.

"Our whole lives?" he asked, a smile spreading across his face.

"Well, maybe, who knows," I replied defensively.

"Hey, you can't take it back now." He gently pulled me closer by my hands. "I want to spend my whole life with you. I love you, Rosie."

Dumbstruck, I stared down at the man in front of me, not believing he could love someone like me. I let myself believe him, taking in this moment. "I love you too, Benny," I whispered back.

"Do you believe in love at first sight, Rosie? Because I fucking do. Since the moment I met you, I haven't been able to think of anything else. Since I held you in my arms in the hospital, I knew it was you." He picked me up and carried me off to our bedroom, celebrating this moment with me.

Ben

It was her birthday; she had no idea I knew and was still fast asleep in our bed with Doug tucked under the throw. I had taken the week off of work; she didn't know that either.

I'd woken early that morning to meet Jim and Mike, who'd arrived with a load of balloons and her present, which they had been stashing at theirs. I had it all planned. Today she would wake up with me, then we'd drive down to the cabin on the lake I had rented for us and her whole family—Simon, Archie, Louis, his wife Rachel and their two children, Bella, who was eight months old and who Rosie had never met, and four-year-old Freddie, who she had only seen photographs of.

I had been speaking to Rachel on the phone whilst planning the trip. She was much easier to chat to than Louis. She didn't give me 'the talk', but did tell me a few times how much she loved her sister-in-law. She mentioned their children, and I suddenly realised how little I knew about

Rosie. I laughed with Rachel that she'd have to give me a family tree to keep up.

Small footsteps headed my way. Rosie was stood in the hallway, stifling a yawn and still rubbing the sleep away from her eyes, only wearing my T-shirt and her fluffy socks that always made her slip over. Her mouth dropped open as she stared at the balloons, bright green eyes scanning the room to land on the 'happy birthday' banner and flowers. Her eyes searched for mine past the balloons and the decorations. She looked at me, shaking her head in disbelief.

"Happy birthday, darling," I said as I walked towards her. She held out her arms, pushing me back as I walked towards her, gripping my forearms.

"What, how … how did you know?" She was shaking her head as her eyes started to brim with tears. Her legs buckled slightly as she leant forward, head in her hands.

I bent down slightly, prised her hands from her face and lifted them up so they stretched around the back of my neck. I lifted her up as I usually did, encouraging her legs to wrap round my waist. She looked into my eyes and smiled through the tears now spilling down her rosy cheeks.

"Thank you, Benny, I really am so lucky to have found you."

I smiled up at her and kissed her gently on the tip of her nose. "I'm the lucky one. Plus, it was me who found you."

She laughed as she pulled my head towards hers and kissed me. I carried her back towards the island and placed her onto the stool, spinning her round to face me on the other side of the island.

"Here, present time," I said eagerly, pushing a gift bag towards her. She looked up at me. Oh, no, she looked like she was about to cry again.

"You didn't have to; the balloons and flowers are more than enough."

I ignored her as I pushed the bag towards her. She smiled excitedly up at me as she lifted the gift-wrapped present out of the bag. She found a small flat square box in amongst the wrapping and lifted it up, her eyes widening. She fumbled with the ribbon, then, trying to steady her hands, opened up the lid of the box. Her mouth dropped open as she looked down with disbelief in her eyes, then looked back up at me. After repeating this a few times, she finally managed to speak.

"Fuck right off."

I laughed. I should have known this would be her reaction. Lifting the dainty silver bracelet out of the box, I motioned for her to lift her wrist as I fastened it round her. The bracelet was made out of a fine silver chain with a small dachshund hanging from it, a tiny diamond placed on the charm, and looked perfect on her petite wrist.

She looked down, examining the shiny bracelet. Shaking her head in disbelief, she looked back at me. "Ben, this is too much, I've never had anything this beautiful." I smiled down at her, not needing her to say anything. I pulled her lips to mine and kissed her. "Thank you," she said between kisses. The look on her face was worth anything to me. I'd give her the world if it would make her happy. I'd move fucking planets for this girl.

She spent the whole of breakfast examining her bracelet, staring down at it as she walked past different lights. She was so distracted by her gift she didn't notice I was packing our bags. I was unable to contain my excitement any more as I held the two bags. She glanced over at me before looking back to her wrist, then looked up again, staring at the bags. "Huh?"

"Get changed, sweetheart, we're leaving in five minutes." I ignored her confused expression as she compliantly headed back to the bedroom. "Casual and comfortable," I shouted out over my shoulder.

She returned from the bedroom wearing her black skinny jeans and a black T-shirt with one of my old plaid shirts hanging off her shoulders.

She put her Doc Martens on and picked up the wiggling dachshund. "Is Doug coming?" she asked hopefully.

"Of course, darling." I smiled down at her, gave her a kiss on her head and him a kiss on his head. The things I did for this girl.

"Mind if we take your truck?" I asked her as we walked towards our cars. Hers was newer and much more comfortable for a journey.

"Sure, can I drive?" she asked eagerly. I laughed, raised my eyebrow, and shook my head. "Was worth a try," she teased as she strapped Doug into the seats in the back, placing down a blanket for him to nestle into.

I came round to the passenger side and boosted her up into her truck. "What?" I questioned as she stared at me.

"We're matching, kind of." She laughed as she looked down at my black jeans and matching plaid shirt.

"Well, darling, that *is* my shirt," I teased as I tugged on the shirt she was wearing, pulling her towards me and planting a kiss on her lips.

We carried on our journey across the other side of the island. Rosie spent the first half of the journey staring out of the window chatting animatedly to me, then started to busy herself again reading. She was still in a different world, immersed in one of her books as we arrived at the isolated cabin.

The cabin was made entirely out of wood and was right on the edge of the lake. We pulled up and I parked the truck next to two other parked cars. Before she had the chance to look up I reached over and covered her eyes, pulled her across the truck and onto my lap.

"Don't peek," I whispered in her ear. She was still giggling as I pulled her with me out of the truck. With one hand I held her up close to me and with the other I lifted Doug out of the back and allowed him to run towards the cabin. I guided her in through the front door, where I saw Archie and Simon poised with party poppers in their hands. A smiling woman knelt on the floor with a young boy who must have been Freddie, both also holding party poppers. My heart warmed as I saw how excited he was, stamping his feet. Louis stood holding onto a small child, smiling proudly down at his younger sister. I turned Rosie to face her family as I lifted my hand off of her eyes.

Rosie

"Surprise!" The sound reached me before my eyes came into focus. I looked round the room as my eyes settled on my family.

I let out an excited squeal as I ran over to Rachel, with a little boy I recognised from photos as my nephew sat beside her. I slipped onto my knees as I ran towards her, trying to get to her as quick as I could.

Her hair was a bright auburn colour, which had clearly been inherited by her children. She had kind, bright blue eyes that were brimming with tears, and freckles painted her cheeks. She pulled me in to her soft, curvy body. She also tried to stand up, so we ended up falling in a small heap on the floor, our arms wrapped round each other.

Rachel had practically raised me. When I was fourteen I'd moved in with her and Louis and the rest of my brothers. She was ten years older than me and had begged social services to take me in. It was her who'd given me 'the talk', bought me my first tampons and taught me how to pluck my eyebrows.

No surprise I cried against her, matching her sobs. I hadn't seen her since I'd left theirs, unable to return. She'd made excuses to come see me at the hospital and had begged me to return to theirs. She'd had no idea how trapped I truly was.

I felt arms round us on the floor. Louis knelt down beside us. Tears fell down his face as he watched his sister and his wife have their emotional reunion. He was a sap when it came to Rachel.

We must have been there for a while before I was being hit with the legs of a Spider-Man bouncing off of my head, I released myself from their grasp and turned to face the small child prodding me.

"You must be Freddie." I smiled, my heart warming at the sight of him. Louis had shown me pictures, but this was the first time meeting my smallest family members.

"Happy birfday," he stuttered back, still bouncing the Spider-Man off of my body. Wrapping my arms around his tiny body, I pulled him in against me and gave him a big kiss on the top of his head as he settled onto my lap. I gazed round the room as I was still sat on the floor. Simon and Archie were staring back down at us, still holding their poppers. They pulled the ends and let the confetti and streamers float over me as I hiked Freddie up onto my hip. I walked over to them and hugged them both, giving them both a kiss on the cheek. I turned back around, still cuddling my nephew close. I had missed so much of his life and I promised myself as I held him close, that I wouldn't miss any more.

I gave Louis a quick hug. "Thank you for being here," I said. He rolled his eyes at me in response.

Ben stood next to Rachel, who was chatting animatedly to him and holding little Bella. I walked over to Simon and gently placed Freddie back down on the floor, where he ran off and zoomed back into one of the other rooms. I let out a laugh, then wrapped my arms round my newest brother. He held me close and didn't let go.

"Happy birthday, Ro," he muttered into my hair.

When he eventually released me, I walked over to Rachel. "Can I?" I asked eagerly, holding my arms out for Bella. She smiled, pausing slightly in her conversation with Ben as she passed me the sleeping eight-month-old. Bella curled her little head underneath my chin and nestled right into my shoulder. In pure bliss, I walked towards one of the sofas and sat down gently, holding her close to me, taking in that baby smell. I loved her so much already. She was so perfect.

I looked up as my eyes locked with Ben's. In that moment everything suddenly felt clear. It felt as if a haze had lifted in front of my eyes, and everything made sense. He stared intensely back at me as I held Bella close. He gave me a knowing nod as I smiled back at him. I knew he was my future.

Everyone gravitated over to the sofas we were sat on, still all talking excitedly, happy to all be together. Louis sat on one side of me, stroking Bella's head absentmindedly. The sofa sank down again as Ben sat on the other side of me, staring fondly at me while I still held a sleepy baby.

Emotions were bubbling up inside of me from seeing Rachel. I felt overwhelmed with love in that moment and burst into tears, unable to contain my emotions any longer. Ever since I had left Jason, my emotions had come to the surface. Years of suppressing any feelings had caused me to turn into such an open book when it came to how I was feeling. Louis looked at me, confused, and gently lifted a sleepy Bella out of my arms and passed her to Rachel, who was now kneeling down beside me.

Ben put his arm around me and squeezed my shoulder. "You're okay, aren't you, you just feeling extra happy?" he said in a conciliatory tone, more for the worried faces around us than for me.

I nodded and smiled reassuringly at my family, who were now staring at me like I was about to explode. They let out small laughs, but all still full of emotion. I wondered if Ben would ever know how much this meant to me, how important this moment was and how important he was to me. He had rescued me, the same as my family had all those years ago. Ben played with my hair as I began to talk.

"It's just been so long, and it's my fault and I'm so sorry, I've missed out on so much. You both did so much for me and then I just left you. I didn't come see Freddie or Bella when you asked me to."

Louis shook his head, anger filling his face as if he was about to start mouthing off about my ex. Rachel placed her hand on his leg, stopping him. "None of that matters, Rosie, we're back together now. We're not losing you again, we love you and we're here. We won't ever lose contact like that again, I just wish we had pulled you out earlier—" She shook her head, then started again. "But we can't go back, we're here now and we will always be your family. I'm so happy you've found Ben. Look at how he's looking at you, he loves you almost as much as I love you, girly," she said, smiling sweetly up at Ben.

His strong hands stroked the back of my neck. "I think I love her more," Ben teased.

"Not possible," both Louis and Rachel said in unison. We all laughed together then sat in a comfortable silence.

That evening I spent time with Rachel and Simon in the kitchen as the others played with Freddie and his Lego. We were cooking Italian food together; Rachel was half Italian, and this was her speciality. The smells were so nostalgic, I remembered all the pasta she used to cook us when we lived with her. Although she was only ten years older than me, she was the closest thing I had to a mother figure. My mum had been useless even before she left us.

Pushing the intrusive thoughts out of my head, I nestled my cheek against Bella, who was sat facing forward in my lap. My legs were crossed on the kitchen counter as I held her close. I couldn't get enough of my niece and nephew. The three of us laughed, drank wine and caught up for hours, prolonging the cooking. Content was the only way I could describe how I felt in this moment.

Ben

I smirked as I walked back into the kitchen and found the three of them laughing together on their second bottle of wine. Not wanting to interrupt their fun, I prised a sleepy Bella up out of Rosie's lap as Simon filled Rosie's wine glass. She was so small, I held her close and started automatically bouncing her up and down in a soothing motion. Rachel was staring at me, smiling, and then looked over to Rosie and winked.

"Told you." Simon laughed at the two ladies.

"Told her what?" I asked.

They all looked me up and down, then let out another giggle. Not wanting to hang about any longer, I leant down and kissed Rosie, then walked out of the room still with Bella in my arms.

Archie met me in the hallway, taking Bella from me. "I'll put her down so they can catch up," he muttered as he walked down the corridor of the cabin. I slipped on my boots, then headed outside towards the decking. Louis was sat outside smoking. I sat down next to him and looked over at the reflections in the lake.

"This was a good thing you did today," he said as he took another drag of his cigarette, I nodded back at him. "Rachel won't let her go all weekend now," he added, laughing quickly before stopping as he looked round over his shoulder.

Rosie had walked out onto the decking and settled onto my lap. He stubbed out his cigarette and nodded as he walked back into the cabin. He was a man of few words, but I appreciated everything he and Rachel had done for my girl, long before I'd had the chance. Curling my arms around her, I pulled her close so she was straddling me.

"You're so happy," I whispered as I brushed her cheek with my knuckle.

"I'm so unbelievably happy it's ridiculous." She grinned back at me. "Thank you, Benny, this is the best day of my life ever, ever, ever," she said, kissing me between each 'ever'.

"I love you, baby," I replied as I pulled her kisses deeper to me.

She giggled and pushed herself back slightly. "I love you too, but we can't do that here." She smiled down at me as she pushed her ass further into my hands, teasing me. "Please come spend some time with us inside. I know it's overwhelming, but I really want you to get to know Rachel and Louis more, they're the whole reason I didn't get put into care when I was younger, they took me in, they took us all in."

I squeezed her bum tightly and stood up with her, letting her legs drop to the floor. I could see how much this meant to her and I wanted to get to know her family. I let her guide me by my hand back inside, where we spent the rest of the evening with her family.

CHAPTER 15

Playing with Fire

Rosie

The next few days were perfect. We spent most of the time on the lake, playing on the water and lying out in the warm sun. Who knew this perfect oasis was just the other side of the island to us? As if he couldn't get any better, I watched as Ben spent time with all of my brothers and made extra effort to spend time with Rachel and impress her with his breakfast-cooking skills.

On our last night, the boys decided to head out to a bar to watch the football. Rachel and I decided to stay back with the kids and have a girly night in. Ben pulled me tight as he said his goodbyes. "I don't want to leave you," he whispered in my ear, holding me close.

"Hey, I'll be fine, we'll be fine, promise." I didn't like him leaving me either, but I wanted him to spend time with my brothers and I had missed spending time with Rachel so much.

We waved off the boys and headed into the front room after first checking on Freddie and Bella, who were asleep in their beds. Rachel walked ahead of me into the room, her arms piled high with face masks, nail varnish and her hairdressing scissors. She had been begging me to let her cut my hair ever since she'd laid eyes on me a couple of days ago. Rachel always used to cut my hair—she knew how to tame my crazy curls.

Rachel was just making her third joke about needing gardening shears for my hair. I rolled my eyes and picked up the bottle of wine and a corkscrew, following behind her into the living room.

"Ooh, grab the leftover cheesecake, I'm starving, I don't have any hands left," Rachel threw back behind her shoulder.

"We've literally just eaten!" I laughed as I headed back to the kitchen, my feet cold on the tiles, causing me to speed up.

I had caught her up before she got to the living room door, my eyes on the goods in my hands, the lemony smell of the cheesecake enticing me. I was wishing I had brought a second spoon when my thoughts came to a halt as I walked into the back of her. She was unusually silent. The absence of any sound pulled my eyes from the cheesecake, which had mashed into the side of the wine bottle.

When I looked up, my heart stopped momentarily and my breathing shallowed. I felt as if my stomach had dropped from my body and my blood had drained. My peripherals were cold. My body was in an instant state of shock. Rachel was frozen in fear in front of me, staring up at Jason, who was perched on the edge of the sofa, smiling up at us with a gun in his hand. The gun that had kept me prisoner in my own home. I'd felt constant fear knowing that Jason was a firearms officer and had access to weapons. He had only shown me it once before for me to understand how serious he was. It had been enough for me to stay prisoner in my gilded cage.

I pulled Rachel back behind me as he stood from the sofa and lifted the gun in his hands, pointing it directly at me.

"Leave," he commanded, looking momentarily towards Rachel, the gun not changing direction.

"No," she squeaked back at him, "please don't do this, leave now and we won't tell anyone you were here!"

"What's the fun if they don't know I was here?" He cocked his head slightly to the left, still manically smiling back at us, the gun not moving. "I'll ask you again to leave. If you don't get those children of yours and get out of here, I will just have to kill you all. Don't believe me? Ask Rosie, she knows I will," he said jovially. I was so scared of him when he was like this—past anger, past the physical beatings I'd usually get. This was worse. "What kind of mother would let her kids die?"

"Rachel. Go. Please," I said, my voice raised, trying to sound as forceful as possible. There was no way I would let anything happen to her. No one else would get hurt because of me.

She looked back at me in desperation, her body shaking. "You have to, for them," I added, knowing that she needed to think of her babies.

She ran crying from the room. I could hear her pulling the children from their beds. This was it. This was the last time I'd see her, the last time I'd see them. My mind went to my niece and nephew before images of Ben flashed through my mind. I wouldn't see him again. I tried one last hopeful glance towards the door as she ran past, waiting for one last memory of my family. She walked past slowly, holding out a written sign, pausing momentarily out of the way of Jason's vision.

I'M GOING TO GET THEM NOW
BE 10 MINS

Giving a fraction of a nod so only she could notice, I turned back towards him, the gun still raised, that unforgiving look upon his face.

"What now, Jason?" I asked him, my eyes still on the gun. "You going to kill me? Just get it over with." Why was I choosing now to be a cocky bitch? I tried to act calm, but deep inside I was secretly begging for him to get it over with.

He put the gun into his back pocket and surged towards me, fury evident in his narrowed eyes. He grabbed the back of my head, pulling at my hair, and slammed my head down towards the glass coffee table. The glass smashed from the impact of my face. I blinked back dazed tears, my head spinning from the blow, my cheek throbbing with pain. Blinking, I scraped my hand across my face, freeing shards of glass, wincing as they pressed into my hands. With my face stinging and wet from my own blood, I prepared myself for another blow as he slammed my head back down and tossed me to the side.

I landed with my back against the sofa. I was numb. He was going to kill me. I had to let him, I had to stop fighting. Giving up, I allowed him to pull me up by the collar of my jumper and force me against the wall. With the back of his free hand he smacked me across my face. My lip split open instantly and my blood sprayed across his face.

"You fucking bitch, you've got your blood all over me," he seethed through gritted teeth. "Clean it up."

I stared back at him whilst he shook me against the wall. I lifted the corner of my sleeve and tentatively wiped my blood from his face. He lifted his knee and kneed me forcibly in my stomach as I lurched forward in agony. This had to be it, I felt as if I was going to pass out with pain. I let myself feel dizzy, slowing my mind. He kicked me again with a forceful impact and pushed me down onto the floor. He lifted his gun from his back pocket, aiming it towards my leg, and with a bang I felt the intense burning pain as his bullet entered my leg.

I let out a shaky scream as I clutched at my leg, blood gushing out of me, soaking my jeans and the floor beneath me. He walked over to me and kicked me hard in the head. My mind went blank and my body finally stopped.

Ben

I had never been a huge fan of football, but seeing how eager Rosie was to have time with her sister-in-law gave me the motivation to be sat in the smallest sports bar I had ever seen. The bar had a woodsy theme. Wooden beams decorated the low ceiling, and four screens filled up the longest wall in the bar, playing highlights from the Grand Prix as well as showing the football.

I brought my frosted beer glass up to my lips, my hand around the thick handle. As I took a sip, Louis's eyes widened and he jumped up from his chair. I turned round to see what he was looking at, or who. Rachel ran towards him through the crowded bar, clutching their babies tight in her arms. She was paler than usual, tears streaming over her freckled cheeks.

"Rach, what is it, the kids? Are they okay?" Louis asked as he examined his children in her arms. Simon and Archie rushed forward, lifting the children away from her tight grasp. Rachel turned towards me, her legs shaking and her breath steadying.

"He's at the house. Gun. He has a gun. He's got her," she stuttered out.

The table went silent. Louis looked over at me. We locked eyes, then stood up and raced out of the bar.

"Look after them," Louis shouted at Simon and Archie.

I raced towards the truck, fumbling with the keys, my hands shaking and my mind racing. Louis snatched the keys out of my hands and pushed me towards the passenger side. I jumped into the front as Louis started the car. We raced back to the cabin, breaking every speed limit and getting caught at every camera, racing away from the bright flashes as we hurried towards her. We had to get there. I slammed my fist down on the dashboard in front of me, anger bubbling up inside of me. Why the fuck had I gone out? I'd only gone to give her time with Rachel. This was my fault, I shouldn't have left her. Should have killed Jason when I had the chance.

"We'll get to her. We couldn't have known," Louis offered under his breath. He could hear the cogs turning in my brain.

"And what if we fucking don't?" I shouted back at him, unable to control myself.

Louis' hand came down on my shoulder. "Save it for him, big guy."

We turned round the corner onto the drive. A distinctive smell met us first. I recognised the smell extremely well—burning. I stared up at the cabin in disbelief. The wooden lodge was in a blaze of fire, the smoke dancing in circles above as the windows filled with a red glow. I leapt from the truck. Without stopping, going straight into work mode, I ran towards the burning house. I felt the handle with the back of my hand. The fire was right there. I ran round the back of the cabin, shouting instructions back behind me. "Call 999, get them out here now!"

Louis already had a phone to his ear, following me round to the back entrance of the cabin.

"Stay here," I commanded and he stopped, staring at me, waiting for my next instruction. I barged through the sliding door of the cabin, through the kitchen. The familiar cloudy smoke filled my lungs instantly. Dropping down to the floor, I crawled through the house, my vision completely obscured as I felt around, hoping to find her.

"Rosie!" I shouted at the top of my lungs, saving every bit of air I could to shout her name repeatedly. This couldn't be happening again, I wasn't going to lose anyone else I cared about, this could not happen.

A scrabbling sound caught my attention. I kept my head down as I stood up and ran towards the noise. I saw a body hunched down by the side of the sofa. Without thinking, I grabbed the shoulders of the body I now recognised as my girl and dragged her out, not checking to see if she was awake. I backed out through the sliding doors and fell back into a coughing heap on the floor, dragging her body towards me.

Louis dropped to his knees in front of her. "Shit," he cried at the sight of his little sister. I lifted my head up, saw the blood and bruising that had already appeared on her face. Her hand was wrapped around her leg. He'd fucking shot her.

"Help me lift her round." Louis reached his shaky hands under her legs, careful to not knock her injuries, whilst I put all of my strength into reaching beneath her arms and carrying her back to the front of the house, still coughing as I took each step. Doug was shaking underneath one of the parked cars. Thank fuck he had gotten out.

The tension lifted slightly from my shoulders. I saw them before I heard them, the blue lights flashing through the trees, reflecting off of the lake. I heard the familiar sounds of my team arriving. Jim came running towards me with the oxygen in his hands. He looked at me, then to Rosie and back to me again, shaking his head and punching his fist into the ground in anger. I lifted the oxygen mask to Rosie's mouth as he returned to grab another for me.

Trent glanced down at me, clenching his jaw as he rushed past with the hose. I pointed to him to get on with saving the cabin, not allowing him to get distracted by us on the ground. Mike appeared beside me as he adjusted Rosie's mask. He worked in silence as he put a tourniquet around her leg, trying to stop the wound from bleeding. The police sirens approached us and Rich jumped out of the unmarked car. He looked at me first, then noticed Rosie still unconscious, covered in injury, her face lit up by the flames of the fire. He took his phone out and began calling it in.

"He won't get away with this," Rich promised.

"Won't I?" A laugh came from behind us. Jason stepped out of the shadows behind the trees, gun still in his hands and pointing towards Rosie, who was lying unresponsive on the ground. "Should have just let her burn," he added, staring at me.

Unable to control myself any more, I stood up and charged towards him, reaching up to grab his gun.

"No," Louis shouted as he raced from behind him, joining in the fight for the gun as Jason tried to point it towards my chest. Using my remaining strength, powered by my adrenaline and hate, I bent the gun to point it facing upright, away from me. In that moment I could only think about my girl, about how we'd found Rosie, how she'd been completely isolated from everyone she loved, how she lay unconscious on the ground in front of me. The sight of her fuelled me to snatch the gun away from him, throwing it across the ground behind me.

Swinging my fist back, without hesitation I slammed it into his face, pulling my elbow back and putting all of my weight into landing my fist repeatedly. I stopped only when I saw her sat up, supported by Mike, staring at me, eyes wide and full of fear. This distracted me slightly and Jason was able to push me back and kick me hard in the ribs.

Falling, I landed backwards with my hand against my ribs, catching my breath. Jason took the opportunity to stand above me and kick out hard, his boot meeting the side of my head. The pain didn't matter, nothing would stop me.

The next thing I saw, Louis had charged at him, taking my place to smash his fist again and again into Jason's face, not letting up, his focus completely on the man who had abused and assaulted his only sister, ruining her life. Louis' rage was now on display and evident on his bleeding face. Rich ran forward and dragged Louis back from Jason, but only after letting him getting a few shots in.

The officer roughly hauled Jason towards the police car. Rich also stepped toward her ex-boyfriend. My breathing uneven, I bent forward and crawled back over to where Rosie was sat up. Unable to say anything, I lay beside her. I reached out for her, needing to touch her. My large hands held onto her trembling thigh. I hoped this would give her comfort, unable to offer her more in that moment.

Her leg jerked away from my touch and she stood up too fast and moved in the direction of where the scuffle had taken place, using all her strength to drag her injured leg behind her. She leant down to pick up the discarded gun from the grass and aimed it confidently towards her ex-boyfriend. Her eyes weren't full of fear as they usually were in his presence. She looked possessed, focused and like she knew what she wanted to do. Her legs were slightly apart, her chest rising rapidly. She was still fighting off the smoke she had inhaled. Her arm was stretched out, not wavering in front of her as she started to speak.

Rosie

"Jason." My voice was barely above a whisper, but I sounded confident enough to draw the attention of my ex-boyfriend and the two officers who were patting him down before taking him away.

He looked directly at me. We both shared eye contact for what felt like a long time before the corners of his mouth turned up.

"Don't fucking laugh at me," I screamed, now louder with my voice starting to waver. How dare he fucking laugh at me? This was it. It all came down to this moment. He would never come near me again. A rage like none other burned deeply, my blood boiling inside my body, causing me to shake, my surroundings darkening and my head swimming with the possibility of a life without fear. I felt so fucking powerful in that moment.

"Rosie." A warning voice came from beside me. My eyes flitted down to Ben, who was trying to stand up off of the floor, his hands clutching his chest.

Not letting him take this from me, I looked back to my ex. "Stay out of this, Ben." I gritted my teeth, my arm not moving from my target.

Another hesitant voice dared to speak up. "Rosie, it's not worth it, he's getting locked up after this, you don't need to be locked up too," Rich said from beside Jason, nervous about my ability to aim. He would just be collateral damage at this point. I envisioned myself firing bullets until one finally wiped that smug smirk off of Jason's evil face.

"She won't do it," my ex taunted from beside him.

I lifted the gun, my arm straight and steady. A smile spread across my face as I pulled the trigger, aiming a shot behind him. The bullet ricocheted off of a tree above his head. I let out a wild laugh at the shocked faces and gasps around me. This was what happened when you tried to suppress all of the hurt, I was out of fucking control. The crazy bitch within me was out. He had created this monster and this monster would be the end of him. I finally understood what Mary Shelley had written about—I was turning on my creator. But this would only end one way.

Ben had managed to stand and was stood leaning behind me, his arm reaching around my waist, trying to pacify me. It wasn't easy to ignore him with my arm still stretched out in front of me; my body naturally melted into his.

"Ben, don't, it's not fair." My voice was low, pleading with the man behind me who was trying to lower my aim. *This isn't fucking fair, Jason deserves to die.*

"Baby, I know, I know. I'm sorry," Ben whispered, sounding equally distressed as he reluctantly lowered the gun.

Pushing myself back, I snapped out of it and turned to Ben, the gun still in my hand. This was it, the fear had vanished. Fearless and powerful, I was finally taking fate into my own hands, taking control.

Looking into his dark eyes, I spoke out loud, not sure who to. "I can't see past today, I can't see a future with him still alive. He has ruined me, he has destroyed my ability to ever feel happy again and he's now able to walk away." My voice was breaking and shaky. Why couldn't they see this was my only option? Why had Ben stopped me? I couldn't walk away from this. With a broken heart and a hopeless mind, I lifted the heavy gun towards my head.

A gasp and a sharp intake of breath. Shouts came from beside me as my brother noticed my intention. He knew I had lived under this dark cloud before; he knew this was what I had always wanted. Ben's eyes were wide, he was frozen, he opened his mouth to speak but closed it again, not knowing what to say. His head shook again, almost as if he was in slow motion.

"Benny, I can't do this any more, not when he's still out there, I can't." Tears streamed down my face as I pleaded for him to understand.

"No, baby, no, you can't leave me, I promise you we will get him," he pleaded.

I heard doors slam and turned around, holding onto the gun. Rich had put Jason into the car, instructing the officer to take him away.

"Nooo!" A guttural scream came from me as I fell to my knees on the floor. Jason had gotten away, I had missed my chance, he was gone.

Ben

Leaping forward, I caught her by her arm as she dropped to the floor. I took the opportunity to pull the gun from out of her hand, apply the safety and toss it to Rich. *What the fuck just happened?*

Finding my voice, I turned to my girl as I dragged her up from the floor, forcing her to face me. "What the fuck are you playing at?" I shouted down into her tearstained face. She looked broken and defeated, but in that moment I didn't care, I was so fucking angry at her. She could have been arrested or she could have—she could have killed herself. I wasn't ready for a world without Rosie. I would never be ready for a world without Rosie. My world started and stopped with her. I didn't fucking care what life had planned for us, but I knew I could manage anything with her by my side. Together. The day I'd met her my world had shone brighter, everything had come into focus. Nothing else mattered.

"Hey, get off her, man." Louis came from behind me and loosened my grasp on Rosie, enabling her to shrug my hands off of her. Realising my grip had tightened around her, I pushed Louis aside and pulled my girl into my arms. We both sank down to the ground, the adrenaline wearing off. She was buried deep inside my heart, but I needed her in my arms too. Nothing else fucking mattered.

Rosie

Two days had passed since the traumatic events that took place in the cabin and we had all moved into a local guest house as we waited for the cabin to air out. None of us really wanted to leave each other, we were all shaken up. They didn't think I had realised, but they had definitely started to treat me differently, each taking turns to stay with me, to protect me from myself.

Ben and I had spent a night in hospital before being discharged the following day. Luckily, I'd only needed a local anaesthetic to remove the bullet and had to spend the next few weeks seeing a physiotherapist. My face would heal, it always did. Ben was fine—he had some smoke inhalation and insisted he didn't need to go to hospital until he realised I had to go too and took this as an opportunity to stay with me.

Now my hand traipsed lazily up and down Ben's hard body. He had barely touched me since that night, treading carefully around me. What he didn't know was that I was desperately seeking any normality, any sense of how it had been before the fire. He lifted my hand with his, wrapping it between his large tattooed hands, lifting it to his mouth and pressing gentle kisses on my fingers.

"Ben?"

"Mm?" His eyes didn't lift from his phone as he answered me.

"Who did you lose before?"

He stopped scanning his phone. His face turned to mine slowly as he lowered his mobile to the wooden bedside table. Pulling me into his arms, he placed a kiss on top of my head, taking a deep breath before answering me.

"My sister."

I paused, allowing him to continue when he was ready. He had never mentioned his sister before, he had only mentioned that he had lost someone.

"She was groomed by one of my father's friends, got into a relationship with him when she was fifteen. We didn't find out till later. He hurt her. Hurt her badly." Ben took a deep breath, his body shaking as he inhaled. I could tell this was a painful story for him to tell. "Me and Robbie fell out when deciding what to do. I wanted her to tell the police, but Robbie was so soft for her, he would have gone with whatever she wanted. She didn't want to press charges, she just wanted to forget. I thought I knew best; I reported it. He found out and he killed her."

It was my turn to take in a huge inhale. I hadn't been ready to hear that, I hadn't expected to hear that.

"It's my fault she died, Rosie. I reported it when she refused to. He knew it was me, too. Locked her in a house, set it on fire. That's how I got this." Ben pointed to the scar that spread down the side of his face. I had never asked; I'd hoped he would tell me when he was ready. "My captain at the time told me to leave, the house wasn't safe, but I didn't listen again,

I wouldn't leave her in there. She was dead by the time I got her out. I killed my sister, Rosie."

Silence occupied the frilly guest house room. Only the sounds of our steadying breaths filled the room. I went to open my mouth, closed it quickly when Ben began to speak again.

"He got away with it; the evidence had burnt with her. A police officer I knew at the time helped me get my revenge, in return for a favour for him."

My body started to shake. The adrenaline was supplying the space. My palms became sweaty against his chest.

"The officer allowed me to kill him, no questions asked. I used his gun and shot a bullet straight between his eyes. I thought it would make me feel better. It didn't."

I wet my lips, trying to ask the question I was scared to know the answer to. "And what did you have to do in return?" My voice was shaky and not as controlled as I would have liked it. I didn't want Ben to think I was scared of him in that moment.

"When he needed a body disappearing, we'd throw it into a fire we attended." Ben shifted my body so he could look directly at me. "Don't look at me like that, sweetheart. They were always bad people, but not enough evidence to convict. Men who hurt their partners. Paedophiles, rapists. I don't feel bad about it."

I nodded as he spoke, finally starting to understand why he was so protective and willing to go to the ends of the earth to care for those he loved. "Okay."

"Okay? Is that all you have to say?" Ben looked back at me, his eyebrows pulling together.

"Do you still do it? The favours for the police?"

"No, I stopped it. As soon as I met you, Rosie, I realised I had a second chance to do something good. I won't do anything ever again to put you or anyone else in my life at risk."

I gave him a weak smile, feeling overwhelmed by everything he had just unloaded. There was something freeing about him sharing all of that with me. He looked lighter too; his shoulders had sunk further into the pillows.

"What was her name?" I asked.

"Sofia." His hand pulled through his hair, something I had noticed he did when he was stressed or uncomfortable.

"I wish I could have met her."

"She would have loved you, Rosie, almost as much as I do."

"I love you too, Benny." Leaning over, I gave him a soft kiss on his lips.

My mind and dreams had all been consumed by the fire, no matter how much time I spent wrapped around Ben, trying to distract myself. How could I go from feeling so content, so complete with my family to fearing for my life so quickly?

Jason had been arrested again that night, this time without bail. Rich reassured us that his trial wouldn't be for at least eighteen months and even then, it wasn't looking good for a release anytime soon. Rich had also removed any bodycam footage of me holding the gun. This gave us some comfort, a small bit, but enough to allow us to try to move forward. We had time—for the first time in my life I knew I had time, time to live, time to finally really live.

Smiling, I looked over at my man, sat propped against the pillows in our guest house bed. He looked up at me and winked, then returned to the newspaper he was reading. Healing wasn't an overnight process, and I was under no illusions that this was over, but sitting in bed with Ben by my side was definitely a good place to start.

How very normal I felt.

CHAPTER 16

Next of Twin

Rosie

Over the past few weeks we had settled into domestic bliss back in Ben's flat. He insisted it was *our* flat, so I took the liberty to add a few touches to make it feel less like a bachelor pad, even though he claimed I was the first girl he had ever brought there. My insecure mind couldn't help but wonder if that was true or if he was saying it to make me feel better.

I brought a variety of potted plants, added a hoard of cushions, and filled Ben's shelves with books I had found in the local charity shop. Life was still looking pretty normal. I had picked up a part-time job at the local police station as their custody nurse. This mainly consisted of blood tests and cleaning up battle wounds before the guilty individual spent the night in one of the cells. Don't get me wrong, I enjoyed it—I worked two nights a week and picked up the occasional weekend day shift—but it had nothing on the buzz you got from being an emergency department nurse. Getting a job was part of my healing process. Rich was the one who'd got me the interview. He owed me. Ben was happy because he knew I'd be safe there.

The job had helped me to find my smile again. I enjoyed the banter with the drunk arrestees and the time I got to spend with my new colleagues. The best part was I worked with Dr Noreen. She was the sassiest doctor I had ever worked with—she looked so innocent, but if one of the arrestees got out of hand, she could definitely hold her own. We spent downtime between patients gossiping, online shopping and hearing all about her family, who were constantly trying to set her up.

After one particularly busy shift, I crawled back into bed beside Ben. He stirred slightly and lifted his arm so I was able to back up into him. He dropped his arm back round me and nestled his nose in my hair. It was Saturday, he wasn't planning on going anywhere for a while. Curling into his warmth and touch, I had just drifted off into a peaceful slumber when my phone rang.

"Sweetheart, please turn it off," he groaned, lifting a pillow to hold it over his head. He was clearly feeling the after-work beers from last night.

With one eye still firmly shut, I pressed the red button and rejected the call. My phone instantly buzzed again. "It's unknown," I murmured as he growled louder at the sound again.

"Put it on speaker," he muttered, voice muffled from the pillow he was still holding over his head.

I answered and quickly put the phone onto speaker. Before I had a chance to speak, the automatic message interrupted me.

"This is a call from an inmate at HMP Callington, do you want to accept these charges ...?" It trailed off.

Ben lifted the pillow, a puzzled look on his face. "He's not at Callington," he responded to my scared expression. I'd immediately assumed it was my ex. Nodding, I dialled one to accept the charge and the phone let out a connecting dial tone.

"Hello?" I asked, my voice full of uncertainty.

"Ro? Is that you?"

"Billy?" I replied, unsure who else this familiar voice belonged to. Ben sat up slightly, confused about who would be calling me from prison.

"Yeah, Ro, it's me. You finally answered. You haven't taken any of my calls! How the fuck are you? I miss you. When you going to come visit your brother, eh?" Billy said, his voice elated.

"Um, Billy, why are you in prison? I thought you were in Australia," I carried on, ignoring the eyes staring into the side of my head.

"Ha! I've been here for over three years; I get out soon though. Good behaviour, you know me."

Sinking back down onto my pillow, I laughed with him. I definitely didn't know Billy for his good behaviour. "I'm not even going to ask. Does everyone else know you're there?"

"Yeah, course. Archie visited me last week and told me you're down on the island now."

Sitting up again, I suddenly felt really pissed off, my voice shaky in my reply. "He knew you were there, and he didn't fucking tell me?" I half shouted, raising myself up further in my bed, Ben growing increasingly frustrated that I wasn't answering his facial expressions.

"Ro, relax, I don't have long. Anyway, I'm out next week, actually, but I need somewhere to say I'm being released to … can I crash with you for a bit?" Billy asked.

"Um, well, I don't know. It's not actually my place." I hesitantly glanced over at Ben, whose eyes had narrowed and wrinkles had formed on his forehead. "Can you call me again later? I'll see what I can do," I added.

"Yeah, of course, Rosie-Posies. Speak to your man. I'm assuming that's what the hesitation is. Love you, bye," Billy added before he hung up.

The bedroom went silent before Ben erupted.

"You going to tell me who the fuck is calling you from prison then?" he demanded, his voice stern.

"Yeah. That's my brother Billy," I said sheepishly, remembering we hadn't spoken much about Billy.

"Another brother?" Ben asked, exasperated, running his hand through his hair. "How old is he?" Ben asked, his voice softening slightly.

"Twenty-four."

"Twenty-four? The same age as you?"

"Yep, he's my twin."

Ben

"Jesus Christ, Rosie. Do you not think this is something you should have told me? That you have a twin? That you have a twin who is in prison?"

"Well, that's not fair. Technically I didn't know he was in prison again," she replied, cringing.

"Again? *Again?* And you want him to come and stay here? I don't know, Rosie, can't we just enjoy being us two, no drama?" I pleaded with her.

Her face fell. She was my weakness; I'd do anything to make her happy. Jesus, seven billion smiles on this planet and I would do anything to see hers.

"Fine." I gave in quickly. I hated seeing her disappointed. "He can stay, on the sofa, for a short while. But if he causes any trouble, he's out. Okay?"

She jumped up and kissed me, thanking me. "You need to relax a bit," she teased as she walked away.

Watching her sashay away, I lay back in our bed. I really didn't need anyone coming in and messing up how well she was doing. We finally had an almost normal relationship. I picked my phone up from where it had been charging and dialled Archie's number.

"Benny boy, what's up?" he answered.

"What did we say about that name?"

"You let Rosie call you Benny, I thought it was okay now."

"Not for you," I replied. "Anyway, what's up with Billy?"

"Billy? Billy who?" Archie answered in a high-pitched and worried tone.

"He called Rosie. She now knows he's been in prison, and I now know he exists." My voice was monotone. I was too hungover to play games.

"Ah, shit, she pissed off at me?"

Right on time, Rosie barged back into the room, jumped onto the bed, and wrestled the phone out of my hand. "Yeah, I am freaking pissed at you! Failed to mention he was back inside?"

"Sorry, Rosie, we weren't in touch when it happened, you didn't speak to any of us and then, to be honest, it kind of slipped my mind. Then when everything kicked off I didn't want to bother you. He's fine, I just saw him." Archie sounded apologetic and a bit guilty.

"Arch, you should have told me. Anyway, he's going to stay here, Benny said it was fine and I'll make sure he stays on track and gets a job and then maybe he'll stay here on the island!" She spoke at a hundred miles per hour.

"Rosie, don't get your hopes up," Archie warned.

"Stop. Just let me enjoy this, please." Her voice was a whisper.

"Okay, we good?"

"Yeah, we're good, love you," she added, then hung up.

Cupping her face in my hands, I smiled up at her, trying to reassure her. She was so excited. If Billy let her down or upset her he'd have to answer to me.

My mind flitted back to the first time visiting Archie's home, the pictures on the wall and the mystery boy I had not met at that point. Hoping this was the final secret between us, I dragged myself out of bed.

Later that afternoon her phone rang again. She jumped up as she listened to the automatic message, quickly pressing one to accept the charges. She put her phone straight onto speaker, a habit we both had.

"He said yes, he said that's fine!" she burst out before Billy even had a chance to say hello.

Billy laughed back at his excited twin. "Excellent decision! He there?"

"Uh, yeah, he's right next to me actually, you're on speaker. His name is Ben and I really love him, so be nice," she added before passing the phone over to me. She gave me a forced, gritted smile; I kissed her cheek as she passed me the phone.

"Hello."

"Uh, hi, I'm Billy, I'm Rosie's brother—well, one of the many," he added, chuckling down the phone.

"Hi." What did you say to someone in prison? Rosie was looking up at me with wide eyes and encouraging nods as she bit down on her lip. "Nice to speak to you, you're welcome at ours till you find your feet." Reaching down, I pulled her lip from underneath her teeth. She gave me an exaggerated thumbs-up.

"Yeah, thanks, man. I know this doesn't look good, but I won't be any trouble. I just want to spend time with my sister. I haven't really spent much time with her since she moved out to be with … er, her ex now. What happened there?" he added, his brain also working at a hundred miles per hour as he changed direction. He already reminded me a lot of Rosie.

Rosie sat up, shaking her head at me. "Didn't work out, Bill, don't ask," she blurted out.

I hated when she kept secrets from people and wasn't honest to try to protect others. They should be more focused on protecting her. She should talk about this; her twin should know. I let her lie to her twin as we said our goodbyes and agreed to pick him up next week.

CHAPTER 17

Hands-On

Rosie

This was the most excited I had felt in a while. Having something positive to focus on was the best thing for me. I spent the rest of the week getting everything ready for Billy's arrival, stocking up on his favourite cereal from when we were kids. I hadn't really spent much time with him in almost six years but wanted him to feel at home, needing more than anything for this to work out so I could have my twin by my side.

I needed to get a few last bits from the supermarket before he arrived. I decided to take Doug out for a walk instead of driving there. We took the slightly longer route, which meant I could stop by the fire station. Strolling through the metal garage door, I put Doug down to allow him to wander around.

"Hey, Dougie man, where's your mama at?" I heard Trent coo.

Laughing, I waved up at him as I walked out from behind one of the engines.

"Hey, doll." He smiled as he lifted me up into the air, twirling me round before dropping me down beside him. "I hear you have a visitor arriving soon," he added, eyeing me, his face hardening slightly.

"Yeah, my brother's coming to stay with us for a little while," I continued excitedly, filling him in on the details. He listened to me, concern still obvious on his face.

"He going to bring us any trouble?" Trent asked after he let me waffle on for a while.

"No, he's not like that. Has Ben been saying things?" I frowned at Trent, disappointed about him pissing on my parade. I was so excited to see my brother, he wasn't this evil person Ben was clearly making him out to be. Ben was way too protective.

"Nah, he's just worried. He's allowed to be, it's part of his job," Trent added.

"Not his job, but whatever," I huffed, rolling my eyes.

"Don't be a bitch about it, Rosie, it doesn't suit you," Trent snapped back at me.

Oh, hell no. I picked up Doug and walked away, not looking back, ignoring him calling my name. *Fucking prick.*

A minute later, I was storming back down the road towards the supermarket as my phone started to ring.

"What?"

"What's wrong with you?" Ben answered back, mirroring my mood.

"Nothing. What do you want?"

"Is this what we have to look forward to with your brother arriving? You being a bitch to everyone? Trent cares about you, don't throw that in his face. There's a lot of people who are worried about you. Stop being such a brat about it."

Shocked that he had the audacity to have a go at me after Trent had ruined my mood, I could only manage, "Right, okay, is that it?"

"Yeah, see you later. Hopefully you'll have a better attitude by then," he said.

"I doubt it." My inner sass queen bubbled up inside me.

"Well, if that's the case, don't wait up."

I clicked off the phone, suddenly filled with regret. This was so petty. After everything we had been through, this wasn't what we needed our first argument to be about. I knew I was being immature, I wanted to be better than this and I was letting myself down. Deciding to not rage-text him, and instead let it go, I continued to swear about Trent under my breath for landing me in trouble.

It was quarter past eleven and he still wasn't home. Checking my phone for the hundredth time, I saw one message and clicked on it, for once feeling disappointed to see my best friend's text.

> Miranda: Hey, girl, where are you? Everyone's here. Ben and all the boys arrived but no you!! Boo. xx

> Me: He doesn't want me there. He having fun? xo

> Miranda: Hmm, bit too much fun, he's wasted!! Everyone is though. xxx

> Miranda: *image*

Sighing, I looked down at the picture Miranda had sent. It was slightly blurry, and I could imagine it was to do with the cocktail she was holding up for me in the photo. Glancing past the mojito, I saw Ben sat at the bar facing towards Miranda, a skinny blonde nestled between his legs.

My heart beat harder against my chest, I felt sick. My stomach dropped and the blood drained from my head. Without thinking, I forwarded the image straight to Ben and typed out a short message, insecurity and jealousy fuelling my spite.

Me: Don't bother coming home, stay at the blonde's.

My phone erupted into phone calls. His name flashed up on the screen four times before I threw my phone across the floor and dragged myself into our bed. I picked up a pillow and screamed into it before I let out a sob, unable to stop until I cried myself to sleep, lifting my knees up and holding them close to my chest. I'd ruined everything. Why did I have to be such a bitch? Instant regret. I knew he'd leave me.

A crash sounded as the bedroom door flung open. I opened my eyes slightly to find three bodies standing above me. Startled, I sat up quickly, pushing myself to the other side of the bed, half asleep and terrified.

"Sweetheart, shush, it's me," a drunk Ben whispered above me. This was hardly reassuring.

"Didn't I tell you to stay at the blonde's?" I seethed back through gritted teeth.

"Darling, please don't be a brat. Nothing happened," he slurred.

Folding my arms across my chest, I raised an eyebrow and stared back at him, scoffing.

"Doll, nothing happened, he's just wasted."

My focus turned to one of the men stood beside him—Trent. "You can fuck off too. You started this, you shit-stirring shithead," I managed, still shaking with anger. *Smooth, Rosie, real mature.*

Standing up, I walked back towards the door of the bedroom. Ben stepped towards me and grabbed my arm, preventing me from leaving. I looked down at his bruising grip, then back up to his face. He was wasted, there was no point arguing.

"Just go to bed, Ben." I felt deflated as I turned towards the sofa, struggling to free myself from his tight grip. Tugging again and panicking slightly, I looked to Trent for support. He effortlessly released Ben's hand so I was able to leave. Walking away, I heard Trent helping him into the bed as footsteps came from behind.

"You all right, princess?" Robbie asked, looking down at me with genuine concern. Pursing my lips, I nodded, but tears started to escape, giving me away. Robbie rushed to my side and pulled me in for a tight hug. He kissed the top of my head, then pushed me back slightly so he could look into my eyes. "Ben didn't do anything, I promise, princess," he said sincerely as he looked down at me.

"Doesn't matter if he did or not, he probably wanted to, he clearly doesn't want me any more." My chaotic, garbled words spilled from my mouth, my self-doubt and insecurities raising their ugly heads yet again.

"You know that's not true; he's just drunk. He didn't mean to grab you either. I'm sure he'd feel bad about that. If he remembers in the morning," Robbie added, shifting uncomfortably on his feet. I looked down at my arm where I had been subconsciously rubbing.

"I know," I whispered. I knew Ben would never hurt me; I knew he loved me, but it did hurt, it did hurt that he'd put his hands on me when he promised he wouldn't. But what hurt me even more was seeing that picture of him. Insecurity would be the death of me.

"What you going to do tonight, princess?" Robbie asked, interrupting my suffocating thoughts.

"I don't want to stay here; have you been drinking?"

"Nah, I only had one. Need a ride?"

Holding Doug close to me, I left without a second look towards the bedroom where Ben had crashed out. It was too late to wake up my brothers, and I felt lost about where to go. Robbie eyed me nervously as he pulled away. He'd left Trent with Ben, thinking someone needed to be there to soften the blow that I had left.

"You can stay with me, it's fine. I'll sleep on the sofa," he said quietly. I could tell he wasn't too comfortable with the idea, worrying about how Ben would react.

"Thank you, Robbie."

Ben

Rolling over, I woke the next morning with the driest mouth and a pounding head. I reached blindly around for Rosie. The bed was empty. Groaning, I lifted my heavy head off of the pillow and reached over for my phone. I searched her name and went to dial. The phone rang out. I went to go send her a text when I saw the messages from last night.

My Rosie: Don't bother coming home, stay at the blonde's.

"Fuck," I muttered as I lifted myself up, checking I was definitely in our home and definitely alone. When I clicked on the image she had sent me, there was a mojito taking up most of the photo. I pinched the screen, zooming into the background, where I saw myself at the bar, the blonde Rosie had referred to standing between my legs.

Shit. I stood up quickly, stomach sinking as I marched through the apartment, hoping I'd find my girl curled up asleep on the sofa. I was disappointed to find Trent stretched out amongst the cushions. Panicking, I pushed his legs so they landed on the floor, lifting the top of his body up slightly as his legs slammed down.

"Where is she?" I was unable to conceal the fear in my voice.

"Huh?" Trent grunted, rubbing his eyes with the back of his hand.

"Where the fuck is Rosie?" I repeated.

"Aw, man, she left after your little set-to in the bedroom. She was pissed. At both of us."

"Set-to?"

"Nothing too bad. You just grabbed her arm, a few words were exchanged, and she got a bit upset." He eyed me tentatively.

My stomach sank. I felt as if the blood had drained from my head. "I put my hands on her?"

"You didn't mean to hurt her, you just wanted her to stay," Trent tried to reassure me, resting his hand on my shoulder to steady himself.

"I hurt her." Shaking him off, I buried my head in my hands. "I shouldn't have ever put my hands on her. I promised her she'd never have to worry about that with me." I sighed, full of regret and remorse. I hated that I'd done that to her. "And who the fuck is the blonde in this picture?" I demanded, shoving my phone under Trent's face.

He grimaced. "You don't remember? That's Annie, you know, the girl from the bakery who's always sniffing around you. She got excited when she overheard you telling us about your argument with Doll face. Sorry, buddy."

"Nothing happened," I interrupted, stating what I believed to be fact.

"True, you just didn't tell her to fuck off. Picture looks shit though." Trent grimaced as he swayed slightly on his feet. "Man, I'm too hungover for this."

Stepping round him, I picked up my phone and started dialling my brother's number.

"All right?" Robbie answered. He sounded slightly pissed off at me. Could hardly blame him. I hadn't drunk like that in a while and he knew why.

"She there?"

"Yep," he replied, his reply short. We hadn't had the best relationship since everything had happened with Sofia. He definitely still blamed me, no matter how many times he had told me he forgave me; I didn't believe him. Why would I? I wouldn't forgive myself. How much he cared for Rosie was the only real reason we spoke to and tolerated each other.

"She okay?" I asked, ignoring his attitude.

"She's okay—upset, tired but okay," he added, giving me a small bit of reassurance.

"I'll come pick her up," I said.

"No, you won't. She'll come back when she wants to. Don't be a dick, let her make her own decisions." Robbie was only being protective of my Rosie, but it annoyed me. I should be the one to protect her, not ever lay my hands on her. I didn't care if Trent didn't think it was a big deal—it was, and I wished more than anything that I could take it back.

"I didn't cheat on her." I tried to refute his attitude.

"I know. She knows." His response pissed me off more. *Is he her spokesperson?*

"I love her," I replied, pathetically.

"I know, but it doesn't give you the right to ever grab her like that. Why would you think that's okay? You forget what she went through, big bro?" His taunts were now testing my patience.

"Tell her I called," I replied before I hung up.

I had to make this right. I hated that I'd grabbed her, I hated that she'd gone to seek comfort from my brother. I hated that I wasn't her safe place. I hated Annie for creeping around me when I was drinking, and I hated that I'd made Rosie cry. That was it though, I was only thinking about myself.

CHAPTER 18

Bakery Battle

Rosie

Deciding to woman up and go back home and face up to last night, I opted for walking to clear my head and get some fresh air. The smell of the bakery distracted me. Lifting Doug, I placed him inside my handbag so I could sneak him inside.

"Can I get a mocha? Takeaway, please," I said to the girl behind the till, not looking at her as I rooted around my bag, moving Doug to get to my purse.

"If you're here to start shit, you should just leave," the blonde girl squeaked out from behind the till.

Huh? I looked up and stared at her. *What the hell? I only asked for a mocha … I knew I should have just got a normal coffee.*

"Uh, any coffee is fine—" It finally clicked as I contemplated a latte. This girl was in last night's makeup, looking rough as hell and terrified of me. Pulling out my phone, I opened up my messages to look at the picture again. I turned it towards her. "This you then, honey?" I gritted my teeth, trying to remain calm and keep the upper hand. *For once in your life, Rosie, be the bigger person. Why am I calling her honey? Sounds like fighting talk. It is.*

"Ben and I had a great night. It's not my fault he's done with you and wants better."

Better. There was that word. I wanted better too. Her voice became increasingly high-pitched so that towards the end of her sentence I could barely hear her. It was probably for the best.

Smirking, I replied, "You're welcome to him, love, but first be a dear and get me a mocha." My tone was sickly sweet. She crossed her arms and huffed, clearly refusing me service.

Tilting my head, I flashed a smile at her.

"Rosie," a stern voice warned. I turned to see who was stood behind me. It was Mike, wearing his tight-fitting uniform. He looked like a damn stripper. I glanced past him and saw the all-too-familiar cherry red of the engine outside. *How small is this island?*

"He sent you in so he didn't have to face both his girls this morning then?" I snarled back, knowing full well Ben would be avoiding the bakery because of last night.

Mike peered at me sympathetically and went to reach out. I flinched and stood back, raising my hands in the air.

"I just want a fucking coffee," I shouted as I stamped my feet. "The bitch behind the counter is refusing to serve me!" I didn't even like coffee, I was just tired and hurt.

Mike's eyes widened as I impulsively picked up the wrapped bakery goods on the counter and flung them over the counter at the blonde, who had already started to throw paper cups at me. This was ridiculous. Doug was cowering inside my handbag as Mike lifted me up and ushered me towards the door.

"You come in here again and I'll get you. Ben's mine now!" the blonde screeched as I was dragged unceremoniously towards the door. I managed to lift a chair fuelled by pure anger and swing it back behind us, landing right in front of the counter, shouting expletives in a haze of rage. I was so angry from last night and this bitch had tipped me over the edge.

Ben

Resting my eyes, I sat back in the engine, rubbing my forehead, still feeling hungover and disappointed that I hadn't seen Rosie before the shift started.

Trent had made us stop by the usual bakery to get coffees for everyone. I needed caffeine, but I definitely didn't need to go in. I chose to wait outside, perched inside the door of the engine, my feet hanging out, allowing fresh air to consume me. Trent, Jim and a couple of others were stood outside, facing me and enjoying the sunshine as we waited for Mike to put our order in.

A crash of metal caught my attention. I saw Mike thrashing around with someone in his arms. The mass of curly hair could only be one person and she just happened to be here—that was karma for me.

"Oh, shit," I muttered as I jumped down onto the pavement and rushed forward towards Rosie. Stepping forward, I instinctively went to go grab her out of Mike's arms. It was taking everything he had to stop her from running back inside the bakery. She was relentless. As soon as she noticed me approaching her, her eyes narrowed and the bright green eyes darkened.

"Get the fuck away from me, don't you dare fucking touch me!" she seethed through clenched teeth. Her eyes had darkened into a full storm.

I stood back, my hands above my head in surrender, feeling useless. I wasn't going to put my hands on her again, not after last night.

"A little fucking help?" Mike panted as he had Rosie in a full bear hug. Sam, one of our trainees, ran forward and grabbed the bag that was hiding Doug to move him to safety. Trent stepped forward, but with one murderous look from Rosie he quickly retreated.

"Ah, for fuck's sake, Rosie, stop this!" Jim took control and marched towards her, grabbing her face gently so she looked at him. "Enough, let it go." He raised his voice, speaking directly into her face. She stilled. Jim stood his ground and didn't move away. I felt a sudden burst of rage watching Jim put his hands on Rosie. She shook her head in defeat and relaxed her body, still in Mike's arms.

Mike loosened his grip from around her waist. "You done? Let's go calm down."

She nodded, still not looking in my direction. She turned to walk away, guided by Mike. All of a sudden, she stopped, dropping out of his grasp, and picked up a loose brick off the side of the nearby wall. She turned and, before Mike could stop her, she threw it at the glass of the bakery.

The glass shattered into thousands of pieces. Annie looked back from behind the counter, completely still, eyes and mouth wide open.

"Oh, shit, she's really done it now." Trent whistled. Amusement filled his voice. The idiot loved chaos.

"Sort this out, we'll go get her out of the way." Jim nodded towards me before rushing after Rosie and Mike.

I turned to look at Sam, still clutching a trembling Doug. "Put him in the engine, out of sight, then come help me clear this up," I instructed; he obliged without asking any questions. I looked at my team. "None of you saw what happened here. This was like this when we arrived, understood?"

They all nodded back at me, all willing to lie for my girl. *Is she still my girl? She may not think so, but I won't let her go.* I strode into the bakery and stood towering over the counter. Annie was crying, tugging at her blonde hair. She looked up at me and batted her tearstained eyelashes in what she probably thought was an attractive way.

"An accident," I commented, not leaving any space for her to reply. Her mouth dropped open as if she was going to argue. What did she expect? Did she really think I'd choose her over my Rosie? "I suggest you go over there and help my boys clean up. I don't want to hear any more from you." My tone was threatening enough so she would get it. She had caused enough trouble.

I walked away and left Trent to deal with her. After we had made the street safe, we headed back towards the station and parked up without the coffee we'd gone out for. I'd had to drive the truck back in Jim's absence.

I'd parked the vehicle in its usual space. Without saying a word, I jumped out and raced towards my office. Rosie was sat in my chair, looking down at her hands in her lap. She looked so tiny in the leather chair. Mike was stood next to her, his arms folded. Clearly, he had been having a few stern words. I didn't know why this annoyed me. Jim was sat in the seat opposite, looking equally stern.

"We quite done here?" My tone was accusatory.

"Yeah, I think so. Don't you, Rosie?" Mike asked, his words sounding almost fatherly towards a clearly remorseful Rosie. He bent down and kissed her on the top of the head and walked out of the office. He patted me on the shoulder as he walked out.

I shrugged him off, then sat down beside Jim. He looked as if he wanted to leave, but I was now blocking his way. "Jim, tell Rosie if I did anything last night, no bullshit."

He sighed, clearly uncomfortable with being there. "He did nothing, darling. Annie has always sniffed around him. We used to always joke about it, we used to get free coffees before we found you. He hasn't even been in the bakery since we met you. He was drunk—wasted, actually— and she took advantage of that. That's all it was, I promise." He reached across the desk and squeezed her hand.

She looked up at him and gave a sad smile. She sank lower in the chair. All I wanted to do was lift her into my lap and hold her close.

"I know he didn't do anything," she muttered under her breath, loud enough for us both to hear. I let out a sigh of relief. Her eyes darted back up to mine; she was still clearly upset with me. "That didn't upset me. Well, not really," she said, fiddling with her sleeve, pulling it up to expose a bruise across her wrist. "You promised." Her voice broke as the tears started rolling down her cheeks.

Jim, still stuck in between me and the wall, looked at Rosie's wrist, then back up to me with guilt plastered across my face, then back down to Rosie. "What the hell did you do?" His voice rose.

"Rosie, I didn't mean to, I'm sorry. I hate myself for that. I never want to hurt you, I won't ever drink like that again. I promise, baby," I pleaded, ignoring Jim, who was shaking his head as he folded his arms across his chest.

"It's fine." She shrugged her small shoulders, still not looking at me.

"It's not fucking fine, Rosie, you should never allow anyone ever to mark you, to hurt you or to ever treat you that way. We know your story, Rosie, when will you learn it's not okay to accept that?" Jim almost shouted. "Now clearly, I know you, Ben, and I know you're a good guy, but you fucked up. I'm going to get out of here before I knock you out. Rosie, I can assure you he won't ever do this again." He jumped up from the chair, stood on the desk, walked to the other side and hopped off, shaking his head as he left.

Letting out a deep exhale, I looked back up at her. She was eyeing me cautiously.

"Rosie, I … I'm so fucking sorry, I don't know what to do," I pleaded with her again.

"I'm not leaving you," she said quietly as she stood up from the desk. "I just really want to go back home, to *our* home, and forget today and last night ever happened."

I stood with her and wrapped her reluctant body into my chest, holding her close until her shoulders relaxed as she lifted one arm up to pat my back. It was a start. The fire bell went off above my head as I heard the hurried footsteps around us, pulling us apart.

"Wait here and I'll drop you home later?" I offered.

She shook her head and smiled as she walked out of the door. "I fancy the walk. Stay safe. I'll see you later." She went to retrieve Doug, who was asleep under one of the sofas, her bag beside him.

"We'll drop you on the way?" I asked, desperate again, not wanting her to be alone.

"Ben, it's fine, I'm okay," she promised, shaking her head as I pulled on my boots. I grabbed my helmet and jacket, then headed back towards the engine. Trent ran past us and squeezed Rosie's shoulder on the way. She shrugged him off but gave him a small smile. They would be okay.

We tore out of the drive. I looked into the mirror as I saw Rosie stood there with Doug in her arms.

"She okay?" Jim asked as he started onto the road.

"Yeah, she'll be okay," I replied hesitantly. "You know I wouldn't ever hurt her."

"I know, mate, but she needs to feel people are listening to her, understand her and are on her side, especially after what she's been through. Plus I am still pissed at you. Don't get that drunk again, you'll turn into your old man."

His words stung. I didn't want to turn out like my dad, ever.

CHAPTER 19

Guilt

Ben

The shift had dragged. When it finally turned ten o'clock, I went to drive home before remembering Rosie had been due to work that night. Knowing my girl, she wouldn't have called in sick—she wouldn't have wanted to stay home waiting for me, especially after today. First, I detoured to the late-night diner and picked up a tray of coffees and a large bag of doughnuts. I wasn't above bribery.

Feeling excited already at the sight of her truck parked up, I walked into the custody reception and greeted the lad on the desk. I hadn't bothered to remember his name.

"You here to see Rosie?" he asked, buzzing me through as I nodded.

Passing through, I greeted the sergeant on the desk. "All right, Greg?"

He grunted back in appreciation as I placed a coffee down beside him, motioning for me to go in through the clinic door. Rosie was laid out on the clinic bed, her Kindle in her hands.

"Quiet night?" I laughed as I walked in, putting the remaining coffee and doughnuts down.

"Don't say that word!" she scolded me. She had told me about how busy work always used to get when she worked in the emergency department and someone mentioned 'the Q word', as she called it.

Swinging her legs off the bed, she beelined over to the goods I had delivered. She picked up a coffee and took a large swig and then busied herself opening the bag of doughnuts. Her eyes lit up as she saw them, then she looked back towards me smiling. "Yum, thank you," she said. Food was definitely one of the ways to Rosie's heart.

She picked up a doughnut, then headed back to the bed, patting the empty space, gesturing for me to join her. She looked so damn cute in her scrubs. They were definitely too big for her—she had inherited a uniform from someone who was much taller. Her legs were swinging off the bed. I sat down beside her, reaching my arm around her and pulling her close.

"We okay, baby?" I muttered against her hair.

"Yeah, we're fine." She leaned forward to give me a chaste kiss on the lips. "I'm so tired." She groaned as she leant her head to rest against me.

"Me too, darling, I could sleep for a year."

"Go back home, go sleep properly. We have a big journey tomorrow and I know you won't let me drive," she mumbled between bites.

"You sure?" I prayed she'd say yes. I was so fucking tired and didn't fancy hanging about.

"Yeah, I'm all right, I'll sleep on the journey," she added, grinning smugly up at me. I gave her a kiss on the cheek, then walked back out towards my car and headed towards bed.

I woke the next morning only when I felt her crawl into bed beside me. She flopped down onto her side, still in her uniform, falling asleep instantly as her head touched the pillow.

"Baby, you need to change." I rolled over and smiled at the sight of her still wearing her uniform, lanyard and trainers. Reaching down,

I pulled her trainers from her tiny feet, then gently lifted her lanyard up over her head. She was dead weight, refusing to help as I pulled back the duvet from underneath her. I pulled off her scrubs and her bra, then I settled the duvet back over the top of her as she slept. Setting my alarm for another hour, I pulled my girl close, holding her in my arms, knowing full well I could never get enough of this feeling.

Rosie

The torturous, horrifying sound of Ben's alarm went off, waking me. I was exhausted, I had only just got home an hour ago. Ben had managed to strip me of my clothes. I chuckled to myself as I heard him in the shower. Jumping up, I stripped off my underwear and headed in there to join him.

"Told you that would make us late." He laughed as I rushed around, hopping on one foot, pulling on my shoe. I winked at him in response; I didn't care. I'd needed that to feel close to him.

Despite our shower, we were early enough to get the first ferry off of the island. It felt weird to be boarding in a car and not walking across in the rain. I took a deep breath as a sudden pang of nostalgia consumed me. Concentrating hard on my breathing, I was feeling anxious about heading back to the mainland.

Ben, noticing my sudden change in mood, squeezed my leg and gave me a reassuring smile. Not able to sit still, I pushed the chair back to full recline and settled myself back as Ben busied himself on his phone.

We arrived three hours later outside of the scary prison gates. Not sleeping had done nothing for my anxiety. This was so shit.

"It will be fine," Ben said, looking over at me as we stood outside the front of the car. I reached out and held his hand, clinging on. The gates clanked as they opened up slowly.

A smiley face and bright green eyes caught my attention first as Billy started to walk towards us, holding a transparent plastic bag over his back. He grinned at us and I beamed back with a matching smile. My shoulders relaxed and my heart swelled, causing me to jump excitedly on the spot. Ben still had hold of my hand. Pulling out of his tightening grip, I rushed over to my twin.

Billy dropped his belongings and ran towards me, scooping me up into a huge bear hug as he swung me round and round. We laughed together as he knelt down, still carrying me, picked up his bags and headed back towards a waiting Ben. He dropped me down to Ben's side and looked up at him. Billy held out his hand to Ben, who shook his hand politely, returning his smile.

"Ready to go?" Ben asked, looking down at the two of us with amusement. Billy had got me in a half hug, half headlock.

"Yeah, get off, Bill," I said as I pushed him off, then bounced round to the front seat.

"Not even going to give me the front seat, eh, Ro?" Billy teased.

"Nah." I smiled back, looking at my brother getting into the seat behind me. Ben started the truck and headed back home. He stayed mostly quiet as me and Bill chatted the whole way home, both avoiding talking about what we had been doing over the last few years.

We settled into a good routine, the three of us living together, it wasn't awkward like Ben had been worried about. Bill was great—he helped out round the house, walking Doug each day. He spent time with Archie and Simon some nights to tactfully give us some much-needed alone time. Billy and Ben had even started getting along, bonding over watching the rugby. Ben didn't fully trust Billy yet, but he could see how happy it made me to have my twin back. He was happy I had someone to spend time with me.

Billy was like me; he got bored easily and not being able to get a job was taking its toll. One evening whilst he and Ben were sat in front of the TV I tasked him with organising the junk drawer beneath the coffee table. It was a job I had put off for such a long time—we dumped everything in there.

"What the fuck, what's this?" Billy called, pulling photos out of an envelope.

Oh, shit. I jumped over the back of the sofa, dived on top of him and wrestled the pictures out of his hand. I snatched them out of his grasp and held them behind my back as Billy reached behind me, trying to snatch them. Ben lifted them out of my hands and Billy stopped grabbing for them.

"Talk. Now," Billy demanded. He held onto me as I turned to walk away.

Ben released my arm as I walked back to the kitchen. Billy ignored him. "Rosie, I'm serious. You tell me now or I'll assume the worst." Billy looked up at Ben.

Ben scoffed back at him, letting out a dry laugh. "Don't even suggest I had anything to do with that." Ben lifted the envelope and passed it back to Billy.

"No, please!"

"Rosie, he needs to know. You don't have to be here for this if you don't want to relive it."

Pausing briefly before deciding to chicken out, I ran towards our room, slamming the door shut behind me. Protecting myself from the oncoming onslaught, I slipped under the duvet, lifting it over my head so I could hide myself away.

About twenty minutes later I heard the door creak open. Tentatively I looked up over the duvet and saw Billy stood there, his face pale and his hand running through his dark curly hair. "Rosie, I …" His voice broke and I shook my head, silently begging for him to stop. I didn't want to hear it. "Why didn't you tell me, Rosie? It's me and you against everything. I thought you just wanted to get away from us, not that you couldn't get away from him … Ben told me everything. Everything," he added as I looked up at him, wincing.

"This is my fault," he mumbled. I looked up at him, questioning his last words. "I introduced you to Jason, he was my friend … I always thought you'd be okay with him. I'm such a fucking idiot. I can't believe I let you down like this," Billy said, his head now in his hands.

"This isn't your fault, Bill." A confident voice came from the door of the bedroom. Ben was looking down at Billy with pity in his eyes.

"He's right, this isn't on you, Bill. Don't be like this. I love you so much and I'm so glad we're back here together." I reached up to put my arms round my brother as I rested my head against his shoulder. Ben sat the other side of Billy and stretched his arm so it went round the two of us. I looked up at him and smiled. He really was the most caring soul.

Billy burst into tears. I froze suddenly, looking to Ben for direction. This wasn't like Billy at all. He was usually so happy-go-lucky and always made jokes about horrible situations. Humour and denial had definitely been his coping mechanisms throughout our childhood. He'd always been the strong one when I fell apart after Mum died.

"I'll kill him, Rosie, I promise you. I will not stop until he is dead," Billy stated. I didn't reply, just held on to him. A problem for future Rosie.

"No, you won't," Ben calmly replied.

"You think I won't?" Billy shouted as he stood up to face Ben.

"No, because I'm sorting it. Just let it go," Ben said with so much finality that Billy just walked away back to the living room.

"Don't do anything stupid, I'm not going to lose you over him," I said.

"It's fine, sweetheart, I promise." Ben smiled down at me. That didn't give me much comfort at all.

Ben

"Bill, can I have a word, mate?" I nodded my head in the direction of the sofa, away from where Rosie was tucked up in bed.

Billy followed me over, his head hanging low, his face still pale from the revelations of the evening. He took a seat, then looked up at me.

"He was your friend?"

Billy took a moment before nodding his head slowly. "Yeah, I guess. We played rugby together. He asked me to introduce Rosie and I did. Wish to fuck I hadn't now." He scrubbed his hands over his face, letting out a low-pitched groan and leaning forward. "He distanced himself from me after I got nicked the first time, just possession, nothing major."

I raised my eyebrow at him. Must have been a lot Billy was holding for him to get time. I knew that and he knew that, but I let him continue.

"Second time, he convinced me to help him shift some gear he'd confiscated from someone, offered me a good cut. Set me up, didn't he. He convinced me to not drag him down with me for Ro's sake. Fucking idiot that I am, I didn't. Took more time because of it." Billy was now rocking slowly in his chair, his hands still firmly planted over his face. He reminded me so much of his sister in this moment. I felt a pang of empathy for how he was feeling, I knew what guilt felt like.

I stood up and sat down beside him, putting my arm around him. "Hindsight's a wonderful thing, Bill, you're here now and that's what's important."

"I wish that's all I'd done, mate. He asked me a few months ago for Archie's address. I didn't even question it, just gave him all the details he needed to come back and get to her." Billy's voice cracked slightly. "I should have known, I should have been there for her."

"Billy, burying yourself in guilt isn't going to help. Trust me, I know how you feel."

He turned his head sharply, his eyes widening in disbelief. "How can you possibly understand?"

I let out an exhale and stood up, heading to the fridge. "We're going to need alcohol for this." I sat back down with a beer in both hands and began to tell him all about Sofia.

A long chat and several beers later, I slapped him on the shoulder and headed off to join Rosie in bed. When I looked back behind me, Billy was gripping his empty beer bottle tightly.

"Billy, guilt is the worst enemy of happiness. Let it go now."

CHAPTER 20

D IS for Drama

Rosie

It had been just over a month since Billy had started living with us. Ben had taken pity on Billy and decided to give him a chance as a trainee on his team. Billy was perfect for the job. He wasn't scared of anything; he enjoyed the risk that the job came with, and wearing his uniform around the island was getting him a lot of female attention.

This new job meant that Billy had been able to move out. He rented a flat in the same block as ours and we were grateful to have our own space back. However, I was relieved my twin was still close. Everything felt better knowing he was nearby.

Ben had tactfully put himself and Billy on opposite shifts so someone was always around. That evening, as Ben was at work, I decided to clean the kitchen, taking out all of the pots and pans and cleaning the cupboards fully. My life really wasn't too exciting. To spice it up, I poured myself a large glass of rosé and left the bottle chilling in the fridge.

I finished my glass at the same time a knock sounded at the door. When I peered through the small peephole, there stood a man who must have been in his fifties, with dark hair with grey brushed through. A dark beard covered most of his face. He was holding onto a can of what looked like cheap cider.

I dialled Billy's number. No answer. I knew he was 'entertaining' tonight. Shit, shit, shit. He knocked again, banging his fist harder against the door until I heard a slump and a thud. I looked back through the hole and saw him sat back against the door. *Bloody hell.*

Ben answered almost instantly. "What's wrong?" I never called, I barely texted him whilst he was at work, so he knew something must be up.

"There's a man here, outside the door, he looks drunk and he wants to come in!" I tried to conceal the panic in my voice, failing miserably.

"I'll be there in five, don't let him in," he ordered as he hung up the phone.

I paced round the room, checking every ten seconds to see if the man was still there. I let go of the breath I was holding at the sound of hurried footsteps. Ben didn't hesitate before he kicked the body of the man on the floor as I listened closely.

"Get up, you absolute mess," he growled at the man, reaching down and hooking him up by his arm.

The man stared back at him, still clearly intoxicated, swaying on his feet. "That's no way to treat your father, is it, Benjamin?"

With a gasp, I pulled the door open, finding myself face to face with the two of them. Of course, it was his dad, with matching dark hair and eyes. Both towered over me as I stood in front of them shyly.

"Rosie, go back inside," Ben ordered. Knowing better than to argue, I went to pull the door back when his dad reached his foot out and wedged the door open.

"Rosie, is it? Why didn't you let me in, darling? We could have got more acquainted," he sneered back at me.

My body froze as I cringed at his remarks. Before I had time to think of something witty to say, Ben grabbed his dad by the scruff of his neck and marched him back down the stairs. "Don't you ever fucking talk to her like that again, you absolute oxygen thief." The venom was clear in his tone.

Listening as he ejected the man, I waited for him to come back into the flat. "Care to explain?" Smiling, I tried to lighten the mood, letting him know I was okay.

"You're not the only one with a waste of space for a father, Rosie. We won't see him again, there's nothing further to explain."

Understanding the need to not have to talk about everything, I nodded, then jumped up into Ben's arms. He lifted my legs up so they wrapped around his waist and carried me back towards our bedroom, a distraction he clearly needed.

We didn't talk again about his dad's visit that night.

Ben

"Sorry, sweetheart, I had to put Billy and me on the same shift, so it means you're coming too, or you can stay at your brother's house?"

She stormed back into the room, staring at me distractedly looking at my phone. "Excuse me? I'm not going to work with you, it's my night off. I'm going to stay in and relax, not go spend time in an on-call room," she growled, crossing her arms and pouting her lips.

"Please don't make this difficult for me. You can't stay here now I know he's likely to pop by again …" I trailed off. We hadn't spoken at all about my dad's visit last week, and I didn't intend on getting into it. I wasn't going to leave her here, it just wasn't an option.

"Why don't I see Robbie? Or he can come here?" she asked hopefully.

Yeah, right. For some reason, the two of them got on really well and it annoyed the hell out of me. "No." This was not an option either.

"Fine, why don't I go hang out with Miranda?" she tried again.

I scoffed. "So you can get really wasted on mojitos and put yourself in more danger? Sure, Rosie, that sounds great."

"Fine!" she shouted back at me and stomped off towards the bedroom. She came back out with her hair pulled up on top of her head and a blanket wrapped round her. "Let's go then." She stormed towards the door, grabbing her bag as we went. She was an absolute whirlwind, a force to be reckoned with when she was in this mood.

I stopped myself from laughing at the sight of her, realising it wouldn't help. Trailing behind her, checking out her ass, I picked up Doug so we could drop him round to Simon on the way and followed my pissed-off girl out of the door.

We pulled into the station and she jumped out of the car before I could come round and open her door. She literally stomped towards the open garage as I sped up to her, wrapping my arm across her shoulder. "Sweetheart, play nice, please," I muttered into her ear. She softened slightly, rolled her eyes and carried on. We walked in with my arm around her. She climbed onto one of the sofas as I went to take handover from the previous shift.

Feeling a sense of doom, I entered my office to find Dina sat behind my desk. I raised my eyebrow at her. She was the team two unit captain and my ex-girlfriend. She never resisted a chance to make me feel uncomfortable.

"Dina," I said, nodding curtly at her.

The corners of her mouth lifted. "Benny, take a seat."

"Don't start, Dina, just hand over." I wasn't in the mood for her bullshit, especially as I had left Rosie sat outside with a unit I wasn't familiar with.

She dragged the handover out for as long as she could. When she passed over the radio, I opened the door and stood against it, beckoning for her to leave. She stood up and brushed her flat ass past me as she left the room. She knew what she was doing. I followed her out to make sure she was definitely leaving.

Rosie had her feet curled up on the sofa and was chatting animatedly to a guy with face tattoos I didn't recognise. "Everything all right?" I interrupted him mid-flow. Leaning down, I lifted Rosie up and sat down where she'd been and pulled her back down onto my lap. Yeah, this was a territorial move. I was making sure he knew she was mine.

Rosie saw straight through my behaviour. She hated when I acted like this, but allowed me to do it, knowing not to make a scene at my work. She looked back at me, smiling as she shook her head. Her new friend stood up quickly, realising what was going on. He lifted his hand in an attempt at a wave and walked away.

"Scaring all my boys away then, Benjamin? Not much has changed, always such a jealous guy." Dina's voice echoed across the garage. Rosie stiffened in my lap.

"You not finished, Dina?" I replied coolly, tightening my arm around Rosie's waist. Purposely ignoring Dina staring at us, I lifted my hand and played with Rosie's curls.

"Who's your new little friend? Flavour of the week?" Dina taunted.

I kept my eyes focused on Rosie as I replied. "This is my girlfriend, Rosie. Rosie, this is Dina, she's the captain of the second unit." I turned this into a formal introduction.

"Nice to meet you," Rosie replied in a polite, but uninterested voice.

Dina scoffed as she looked down at Rosie. "Yeah, nice to meet you, I doubt I'll see you around here again."

"Why's that, D?" Rosie replied, staring up at Dina. *Oh, shit. There's that temper.*

"It's Di-na, darling, and because by our next handover I'm sure your boyfriend will have moved on to the next whore. That's your normal style, isn't it, Benjamin?"

"We all good here?" Mike asked as he joined the crowds gathering around us.

"Fine," I said, "D was just leaving." Rosie laughed as she heard me refer to Dina as 'D', just as she had. Pulling her closer to me, I kissed her neck.

"Fuck you, Ben, and your little tramp," Dina hissed at the two of us, clearly embarrassed now a crowd was forming.

I would have felt more empathetic for her reaction at seeing me with someone else, but I wouldn't tolerate the way she spoke to Rosie or belittled me in front of my crew. I stood up, shifting Rosie off of my lap as I towered over Dina. "Leave. Your shift is over."

Without hesitation, she stepped forward. I laughed to myself as I turned around, shaking my head.

Rosie had stood up and stepped towards her. I caught her round the waist before she reacted. I loved that she was feisty, but I didn't fancy seeing it again so soon.

"Time to leave, Dina," Mike said as he steered her out towards the exit by her elbow.

"Bye, D!" Rosie and I both called in unison, laughing together as we fell back onto the sofa. I put my hand on the back of her head and pulled her towards me in a passionate, possessive kiss. Realising we still had a crowd gathered around us, I lifted her up over my shoulder, ignoring her protests and giggles. As I carried her towards my office and away from the peanut gallery, I lifted my middle finger back to the boys behind me, who had started whistling and hooting, knowing full well what we were going to do. Work would have to wait, a perk of being the boss.

Rosie

We came back out to the main garage. I blushed as I looked up to see Billy sat uncomfortably on one of the chairs, shaking his head at me.

"Oh, hey, Bill," I greeted him, trying to act calm, as if Ben hadn't just had me bent over his desk. "Forgot you were working tonight."

"Don't 'hey, Bill,' me," he replied, eyebrows raised and burying his head back in his magazine. Not hanging about, I walked past him, deciding to hide from any awkwardness in the crew kitchen.

"Hey, Ro," Jamie called as I entered the kitchen. Jamie was employed to cook the meals for each team. He was my age and an aspiring doctor. He was using this job to make himself study during downtime and to earn some money this year before university started.

"What are you cooking tonight? Smells lush," I said as I hopped up onto the counter so I could sit beside him.

"Spaghetti Bolognese." He smiled back. "My mum's recipe."

I helped myself to some grated cheese that was beside me as I continued to watch him cook. I picked up one of his big books and began to quiz him. We enjoyed spending time together; I liked listening to his dreams of medical school and he enjoyed hearing about my stories from the frontline. We were both sat up on the counter reading from the same book as we discussed the difference between paracetamol in IV and oral form when Ben walked in.

"There you are, I wondered where you'd got to." He eyed us both sat up on the counter. "Dinner ready then?" He looked pointedly at Jamie.

Lifting the book, I jumped down from the counter, walking directly over to Ben as I swung the book into his side. "Don't be a dick!" Why was he such a bloody caveman? As much as his possessiveness was sometimes a turn-on, seeing him being mean to someone like Jamie just made me want to punch him in the balls.

"I'm not, everyone's hungry and you're both in here reading together," he said defensively.

"The food is cooked, we stopped for five minutes, I said don't be a dick!" I said as I swung the book into his side again.

He caught it this time and handed it back to Jamie. "Sorry, Jamie, just hungry," he apologised. Jamie ignored him and returned to the stove. Sighing, I gave Ben a look and returned to help Jamie lift plates out of the warmer. I picked up the cutlery and carried it across to the table.

"Hey, this isn't your job, Rosie, you don't have to help him," Ben said quietly, so only I could hear.

"So I can't help him? Stop being like this, just be kind. What's wrong with you?" I whispered, trying to keep my tone hushed.

"I am kind. I let him study when he's meant to be doing other things."

"Right, well, just be a bit kinder. I like him."

"Okay, darling, I promise I'll be nicer to your boyfriend." Ben didn't even attempt to hide his jealousy.

"For that, you can grate more cheese. I ate most of it, can't stop eating." I rubbed my stomach as I dragged him towards the grater. I had a bad feeling why.

Jamie looked over at him grating the cheese, turned slightly, and chuckled as he locked eyes with me. I gave him a wink, then continued setting the table.

We all had dinner together, then Ben and I settled into one of the bunks in the on-call room. He wrapped his arms around me as I drifted off to sleep.

I woke a couple of hours later as I heard the alarm bell. Ben jumped up automatically, leant down to kiss me then left the room. I knew the drill—the alarm sounded and he went. Jamie stayed overnight also, he was in the opposite bunk room, so I didn't feel alone. Rolling over, I drifted back to sleep, my belly still full of Bolognese and God knew what, my mind at peace.

I was rudely awoken by a fist slamming down into my face. "What the—?"

Another hand clutched the neck of my T-shirt. I tried to sit up, still stunned and completely disorientated. Another blow pushed me further into my pillow. A wetness dripped onto me from my nose. Slowly opening my eyes, adjusting to the darkness, I attempted to lift my hand up to push my attacker away when she came into focus.

Dina. The crazy bitch stood over me in a full rage, raising her arm back and landing another punishing blow to my face.

"What the fuck are you doing, you fucking psycho!" I shouted as loud as I could, hoping to wake Jamie next door. It worked. I was being pinned down by her on top of the bed when he ran into the room in only his boxers. He raced forward to grab her off of me. She pushed back hard and he tripped over the bunk behind him, hitting his head and stumbling backwards, knocked unconscious. *For fuck's sake, really?*

She was momentarily distracted, and I managed to push her hand off of my neck where she was slowly choking me. I slipped down off of the bottom bunk and stood up shakily so we were level. Swinging my arm back, I slapped her across the face. She paused, holding onto her cheek, then pushed me against the bunk, my head slamming into the metal. She grabbed me by the back of my hair and pushed me down, kneeing me in the stomach repeatedly.

The pain was like no other. My mind went straight to my stomach. I hadn't got my period the last couple of months and this morning as I'd accidentally pulled a tampon from my bag, the other shoe had finally dropped. There was an unused pregnancy test in my bag that I would never have the chance to use. She was going to kill me and my potential baby. Feeling attached to the possibility of something half me and half Ben, I prayed to a god I did not believe in that I would survive this.

Ben

We pulled back into the garage, noticing another car had arrived. Something felt off. I looked over at Jim, who looked perplexed. We jumped out of the engine and started unloading the equipment. We had been called out to a hoax call, so all of us were extremely tired and pissed off.

We started our debrief when we heard a loud clang from the metal bunks. Not hesitating, I ran straight towards them, looking for my girl. I wasn't prepared to see what I saw—Jamie unconscious in his boxers on the floor and Dina beating on Rosie, Rosie not fighting back, her eyes completely vacant. Blood stained her face and ran down her T-shirt. Her eye was already swollen shut.

I rushed forward and grabbed Dina, pulling her back. She fell with Rosie's thick hair still entwined in her hands.

"Help," I shouted. My team had already arrived. Mike was pulling Jamie to his feet and Trent dived past me, pulling Dina's hands from Rosie's hair. "Get rid of her, call the police," I shouted as Trent and another lad pulled her out of the room, Dina still fighting back in a full-blown rage. Kneeling to the floor, I lifted Rosie into my lap. Her body was limp but she was still awake. She was scaring me.

"Rosie, baby, come back to me. It's okay, she's gone, I'm here," I whispered to her, rocking her in my lap. Jim knelt down beside us and helped me to lift her up so she was sat down. He leant her head forward and pinched her nose in an attempt to stop it from bleeding. His other hand stroked her back in a soothing rhythm.

Billy was stood in the doorway, his fists clenched at the sight of his twin. He hurried back round to hunt down Dina, who was being restrained by three people. She was a strong fucking bitch. Knowing Rosie was safe with Jim, I followed Billy into the main room. Billy strode straight over to Dina and spat in her face.

"Enough," I declared, my protective hand on his shoulder. I dragged him back, not wanting him to get in any trouble. He turned round and looked at me, his jaw tense and his fists still clenched. "Go back and be with your sister, she needs you," I insisted, trying to distract him.

He marched past me. You could almost feel the steam coming from him. I knew I should have gone back to Rosie, but I couldn't bring myself to see her like that right now. Making sure Billy had left, I approached Dina.

"Now, D, I'm going to call the police, they'll arrest you for assault and naturally you'll be fired. If I ever see you come near me, my station or my girl again I won't be so kind, got it?" I threatened. She glared back at me, silent.

"I asked you a question," I seethed, awaiting her response.

"I got it," she muttered, looking down at her feet.

"You got her?" I asked Trent. Trent nodded, eyeing me cautiously, and pushed Dina back into a chair in front of him.

I stormed back through the station looking for Rosie. I found her sat beside Mike as he applied a dressing to a cut on her cheekbone. The vacant look had disappeared, but she clutched at her stomach, leaning forward and whimpering in pain. Mike asked the others to get out of the room. Jim walked by with his arm around Jamie, who was clearly shaken up by what had happened.

Mike asked Rosie to lift up her T-shirt so he could see her other injuries. Her stomach was already bruised and she clutched it tightly. We helped Rosie to stand up so he could have a look. She hunched over and let out a whimper, unable to straighten up.

"Something feels weird," she said through gritted teeth, looking directly at Mike.

"Ben, can you give us a minute?" Mike said, helping Rosie back down.

"No, what's going on?" I asked as I got closer to Rosie, sitting beside her on the bunk, wrapping my arm around her.

"Rosie, do you want him to leave?" he asked, not looking at me. I stared directly at him. What was he trying to do?

"Yeah, Ben, please just leave for a second. I'm fine, please just give me a minute." She winced, shrugging off my arm.

"I'm not going anywhere," I proclaimed, looking between Mike and Rosie. "Tell me what's going on now."

Mike looked up at Rosie apologetically as she let out another squeal, leaning forward and clutching at her stomach.

"It's fine, stay, I just want the pain to stop, please," she said deliriously. Her eyes rolled back slightly as she looked like she was about to pass out. A patch of blood on her watermelon pyjama bottoms caught my attention as I moved closer.

Billy piped up from the corner he was standing in, clearly pained by seeing his twin like this. "Is she pregnant?" he questioned quietly, but loud enough for us all to hear.

"I think so. Would explain the bleeding," Mike sighed, supporting Rosie to sit comfortably. "Rosie, angel, could you be pregnant?" he asked her, avoiding my eye contact.

I felt bile rising from my stomach. *Was* she pregnant? If she was, why was she in so much pain? Why hadn't she told me? She gave a fraction of a nod as tears escaped her eyes, then slumped down off the bunk and onto the floor, curling her legs up in agonising pain.

I knelt beside her and looked up at Mike. "What the fuck do we do?"

"We have to wait for an ambulance. I've called one already."

"Do something," I begged him.

"I can't do anything, Ben, we just have to wait, I'm sorry," he cried, shaking his head.

Billy knelt down in front of his twin and got down onto his side facing her, reaching out to stroke her face as more of her tears escaped. He was feeling her pain too. I couldn't watch her as the tears streamed down her face, her breathing shallow and her hand guarding her stomach. She was pregnant. I shook my head, trying to focus myself on what to do next.

"The ambulance is caught up with another patient, they're not going to be here for a while," Mike whispered, wincing as he looked down at Rosie on the floor.

Rage forced me back into the garage. Jim grabbed hold of my arm again before I let out my anger on Dina, using her as a verbal punching bag. "Stop," Jim said. "Let's take Rosie in the engine. Go get her, I'll start it up."

It worked. It distracted me fully as I ran back into the room and explained the plan to Mike and Billy. Everyone cleared a space as I carried her out in my arms, their expressions scared and confused. Trent ran forward and opened the door for me as I lifted Rosie into the back seat, sitting beside her. Billy and Mike jumped in behind me, but as Trent went to get in, I stopped him.

"No, I need you to stay here and make sure Dina is dealt with. Come see us after the shift ends. You're in charge."

He looked momentarily upset about not being able to come with us, but nodded and cleared everyone out of the way of the engine, allowing Jim to flick on the blue lights and drive away.

We arrived outside the front of the hospital, the siren of the fire engine alerting the hospital we had arrived. A few members of staff in scrubs looked confused, expecting an ambulance. We jumped out of the engine. I was still propping Rosie up. I lifted her up and placed her onto the trolley they had dragged outside. After a quick pause they wheeled her back inside, firing questions off to us. I was grateful Mike was there to answer them. My mind was numb. We were back to where we'd started. I couldn't see her in a hospital bed again.

Unable to follow anything further, I allowed Mike and Billy to rush forward. Jim put his hand on my shoulder. I turned towards him, looking for answers. "What do I do? I can't put her through anything like this any more, this is my fault."

Jim sighed and looked sympathetically at me as he steered me towards a row of chairs. I sat down, my head in my hands.

"Look, mate, that doesn't matter now. She may or may not be pregnant with your child. Nothing matters apart from that. Now you go in there, put your bullshit behind you and suck it up for her."

He was right, this wasn't about me. I walked towards the doors that they had taken Rosie through. She was sat up on one of the uncomfortable trolleys, holding her knees close, her chin resting on top. Her eyes widened as she saw me approaching. She had an IV running into her hand and she looked much more relaxed. I kissed her on the top of her head, using my hand to rub circles on her back.

"What's the plan?" I directed my question to Mike.

"They've made her comfortable and then they're sending her for a scan. Trent has called also. Dina's been arrested."

"Why are they taking so long?" Billy muttered under his breath; he was frustratedly pacing beside the curtain. Billy couldn't sit still at the best of times.

We waited there in silence for another twenty minutes until a porter arrived with a wheelchair to take Rosie to her scan. The porter spent time fumbling around with the bed, trying to lower it to the chair. Getting impatient, I lifted Rosie effortlessly from the bed and into the chair, careful to not knock her IV. A smiling nurse rushed forward and disconnected her, allowing Rosie to be wheeled away.

"Only one person," the porter said in reaction to all three of us following. I stepped forward without looking around at the other two. There was no way I wasn't going in there.

When we got to the scan room I lifted Rosie up from the chair and onto the bed. The technician looked disapproving at this breach of manual handling processes. As if I cared. I needed any excuse to touch her. I could have lost her.

Standing beside the bed, I took hold of Rosie's hand. She looked up at me and winced as the technician performed the internal scan.

"Right, that's all done. I'd say you're about nine weeks along, want a picture?" The technician was clearly bored.

"Wait, what? There's a baby? They're okay?" Rosie asked, breaking her silence.

"Yeah, baby looks fine. Looks like there's a bit of damage here, which a doctor will want to follow up at your next scan, but baby looks good. Listen to this." The technician reached for another attachment, squeezed jelly onto Rosie's bruised stomach, then gently pressed down. Rosie winced again, but waved her hand to silence me as I started to protest.

A loud drumming noise filled the room. A heartbeat. That sound that before today I wouldn't have considered a possibility became the most beautiful thing I had ever heard. Rosie gazed up at me, tears in her emerald eyes. Staring back down at her, my mind flooded, I was emotional, relieved. She was pregnant, with *our* baby. Choking back my emotion, I leant down and kissed her, the heartbeat drumming around us.

Rosie clutched hold of the pictures as they wheeled us back round to the desk to book in our follow-up appointments. The porter started to wheel her back. "Hey, let me do that," I offered as I reached over and grabbed the chair from his leathery hands. I needed to hold her. Before we returned to the bay, I wanted to soak up this moment with her. I pushed the chair against the wall and turned her to face me. I knelt down and stared into her eyes.

"We're doing this, baby?" I scanned her face with a full smile on my face, holding on to her knees.

She nodded and smiled widely. "I think so. I'm sorry I didn't talk to you. I wasn't sure if I was, I hadn't done a test yet—"

"Hey, it's okay. All that matters is what happens now. We're doing this. I love you and I'll love them so much," I gushed as I lifted my hand and pressed it gently across her stomach. She leant forward and kissed me, a passionate kiss that was ended too quickly by the sound of hurried footsteps approaching.

"They said you've been discharged. Are you okay?" Billy asked as he approached us.

"We're great, I'm great, he's great, baby's great," Rosie said, beaming and holding up her scan pictures to her twin. He looked back down at her and, with an exhale, releasing the tension he had been holding, he shook his head and bent down to hug her, lifting her slightly out of the chair.

"Fucking hell, Ro, I was so worried. Oh, shit, I'm going to be an uncle," he cheered, wiping an escaped tear away from his face before anyone could notice.

"Congratulations, man," Jim said, pulling me in for a hug.

"This baby is going to have lots of uncles." Mike laughed. "Congratulations, angel," he added as he gave Rosie a kiss on the cheek and a light hug, careful not to hurt her.

"Come on, let's get you back, lots of people waiting to see how you are." I smiled as I lifted her up and carried her out in my arms. She giggled as she nestled into my neck. I had never felt so complete, carrying the love of my life as she carried our baby.

CHAPTER 21

Mamma Mia

Ben

It had been three weeks since we'd found out about the baby. Since the news, I had seen a shift in Rosie. She was eating better, making sure she didn't skip meals. She was reading antenatal books and signing us up for classes. It was as if she had matured overnight. Having something so precious for her to look after gave her a new focus, a new outlook on life, and she had never looked better growing our baby.

"That little shit," I swore under my breath, looking down at my phone.

"What's wrong?" Rosie asked, peering round my arms.

"Robbie told my mum about the baby," I said, sighing and automatically running my hand through my hair.

"You've never really mentioned her before," Rosie replied, looking confused.

"She left us when we were young, couldn't cope with our dad, but apparently we could. Can you imagine ever leaving a nine- and an eleven-year-old to deal with an alcoholic? What kind of mother does that?" I questioned, my voice rising to the point of shouting out those final words.

Unfazed by my shouts, Rosie sat back down, rubbing her tiny bump absentmindedly. "So, Robbie talks to her? Can't be all bad."

"What about what I said didn't sound bad? She abandoned us. Robbie is an idiot, a pathetic idiot who has been roped back in by her."

"Don't raise your voice at me," Rosie warned, raising her hand at me.

"I'm not, I'm sorry, it's just—"

"I get it, Ben, but calm down. She may be the only grandparent this baby has. If she's not an alcoholic, not addicted to drugs and not got severe mental health concerns, then she's winning compared to the rest. Give her a chance. Or don't, but if she wants to be involved, I will give her a chance. Come on, what happens *now* is what's important, remember."

What she said made sense, but I couldn't listen to it any more.

"You can do what you like, Rosie, you always do." It was one of the things I loved most about Rosie—she knew her own mind—but it was also something that caused us both to clash, we were both so stubborn and strong-minded.

Seemingly unperturbed, she rolled her eyes, then busied herself in a book.

Rosie

Robbie and I sat in a comfortable silence in the only decent Italian restaurant on the island. We had already waited half an hour and my stomach growling was the only thing disturbing our silence.

"Sorry, princess, maybe we should order?" Robbie suggested, looking down at my stomach then glancing down at his watch for the fifth time. Not waiting for another invitation, I caught a waiter's attention.

"Some wine to start?" the waiter asked, smiling down at me.

Ha, if only. I would be an idiot to not acknowledge that drinking had been an escape for me, my way to block the outside world out. Everything had changed the day I'd seen that heartbeat flutter on the screen. I wasn't going to let this baby down.

"Hi, no, thank you. Could we order some garlic bread, please? Or mozzarella sticks. Ooh, or the burrata. Actually, no, let's go for the caprese salad."

The waiter's pen was poised above his pad. He was still confused to what I was ordering.

"All of the starters, please," Robbie said, chuckling at my indecisiveness.

"Robbie, maybe she got the wrong day?"

Robbie had been in touch with his mum only via text and phone calls. It had been twenty-three years since he'd last seen her.

As if she heard us, a woman with long dark hair edged through the restaurant, stopping to ask the hostess a question. They both turned and pointed towards our table. It must have been her. Thankfully she hadn't flaked—that definitely wouldn't help Ben's opinion of his estranged mother.

She rushed over to us as Robbie stood from the table and walked into his mother's open arms. They both stood holding each other as our waiter returned with our order. He sidestepped around them and I motioned for him to put the food in front of me. Pregnancy allowed me to eat two mozzarella sticks before they ended their embrace. It wasn't rude if I was pregnant, was it?

They both tore apart from each other, wiping their eyes and laughing. Robbie pulled out a seat for his mum, then returned to sit next to me. "Oh, shit, sorry. Mum, this is Rosie, Ben's girl."

I smiled up at her as she reached out to place her hand over mine, which was heading towards the garlic bread. I imagine she thought it was a handshake. We did a weird handhold over the table. "It's so great to meet you, lovely, I'm Marie." She beamed at me over the table. "Congratulations, darling, Robbie told me you and Ben are expecting."

"It's lovely to meet you too, thank you for letting me crash your lunch. Ben's working, I'm afraid."

Robbie scoffed from beside me.

"It's okay, I know he's not ready yet. Rosie, I made some mistakes—" she started.

I raised my hand. "Please don't explain yourself to me, I get it. I get what it's like living with someone like that and not being able to think straight."

"What do you mean? Is Ben drinking? Robbie, you told me he'd stopped all that." Her voice rose at the end of her sentence the same way her sons' did.

"No, not Ben. Ben doesn't drink much. He's a good egg," I said, wondering what she was referring to that Ben had 'stopped'.

"You okay, princess? You look kind of pale," Robbie questioned, finally giving me eye contact.

My body had started to feel warm and shaky. I felt disgusted by the amount of food I had consumed. "Excuse me." My hand was firmly over my mouth as I hurried away towards the bathroom.

Twenty minutes later I returned to the table, sliding the plates of food away from me, the thought of them churning my stomach once more. Letting out a shivering sigh, I held my head in my hands.

"Darling, maybe we should take you back?" Marie offered gently. She was very maternal for someone who hadn't been around her children for a while.

"Yeah, princess, I'll drive you home."

"No," I said, shaking my head, "please don't. Stay, enjoy your meal. My lift will be here soon." Waving my hand in dismissal, unable to raise my head, I pushed away the garlic bread that was taunting me. A whiff of this as it passed my nose triggered me to jump back up and run towards the bathroom.

Ben

Rosie: Please can you come pick me up? Feeling sick.

Ben: Leaving now.

Feeling increasingly regretful for leaving Rosie alone at lunch, I walked quickly through the atmospheric restaurant, greeted by the hostess with the fake Italian accent. I ignored the hostess, focusing on getting to Rosie. Taking a calming deep breath, I stopped in my tracks when I saw Robbie eyeing me nervously. The woman he was with turned around. It was her.

"Where is she?" My question was only aimed towards my brother. I chose to not acknowledge my *mum*.

She scanned my face hopefully. If she wanted a happy reunion, she wouldn't fucking get it.

"She's not feeling very well, love, she's in the ladies'. I'll go check on her," Marie offered as she jumped up from the table, trying to make herself useful.

I only rolled my eyes back at her as she left. Bit late for the caring, nurturing side to be showing.

"Give her a break, she's here and she wants to be involved," Robbie snapped.

"Until she leaves again," I replied, smiling sympathetically down at my gullible brother.

Marie returned to us without Rosie, worry etched across her face. I didn't wait to hear what she had to say. I walked straight past her and into the ladies' toilets. They were empty, apart from one cubicle where Rosie sat with her back against the stall wall, trying to steady her breathing. I leant over her and flushed away what was left in the toilet bowl.

"Hey, baby," I cooed, brushing her hair back from her face. She was pale and clammy. "Let's get you home." Helping her to stand, I guided her out back towards the table. Don't get me wrong, I loved that baby cooking inside of her, but damn, did I hate the way it made her feel.

"Sorry for ruining lunch, really nice to meet you, Marie. Bye, Robbie," Rosie squeaked.

"Bye, princess, let me know if you need anything."

Rosie was starting to pale again and darted towards the exit of the restaurant. She managed to get outside and into the car park before she started being sick again. I held her by her shoulders to support her as she leant over. For some pointless reason Robbie and Marie had followed.

"What?" I snapped as they watched as Rosie.

"We just want to help, sweetheart," Marie said tentatively.

"Don't fucking talk to me," I shouted as I pointed my finger towards her.

"What's wrong with you? Do you want her to leave again? Is that what you want?" Robbie shouted. We had both inherited tempers.

"Robbie, I'm warning you," I growled, still supporting Rosie, who in between heaves was using her hands to try to shut us both up through hand signals.

"What are you going to do, Benny? Are you going to off me? Going to get rid of your brother, are you?" Robbie taunted.

With one hand I grabbed the collar of his coat. He pushed me back forcefully. I struggled to balance Rosie in my arms.

"What the fuck are you playing at?" I gestured towards Rosie.

Marie ran forward, pulling Rosie out of my arms. I was reluctant to let go, but I also wanted to kill my little brother, so was grateful in that moment. I let Marie pull her down to the ground and sit her up on the kerb.

"Ben, stop, please," Rosie squeaked from somewhere below me.

Marching purposely forward, I grabbed Robbie and swung for him just as he ducked, then he ran towards me, using his full weight to push me into the side of the truck. Retaliating, I grabbed him by his clothes and turned him around so his back was now facing the car and landed a punch into his smug face.

"Boys, stop, please! Oh, God, Rosie darling," Marie screeched as I went to land another punch in my brother's taunting face.

We both turned to look at Rosie, who had lain back exasperated onto the pavement, her hands over her eyes, trying not to throw up but also clearly pissed off seeing the two of us fight. We had more in common than our temper; another was how much we loved Rosie. We both walked over to her in unison and stood either side, helping her to stand up.

"Please stop, I can't fucking stand this any longer. Make up and get over it! Ben, just be nice to your mother. I know what she did was messed up." She glanced over at Marie. "Sorry, Marie, but you did fuck up." She turned back to us both. "You should be grateful you still have a mum and she's a nice lady and she wants to make things right, and if she fucks off again I will personally cut her out of all of our lives."

All three of us stood staring at Rosie after her outburst. Clearly the pregnancy had her hormones racing.

"And I need a fucking burger." She stormed off towards the truck and climbed into the passenger seat.

We all continued to stand awkwardly in silence, looking equally amused at my girl, who had suddenly got her appetite back.

"She seems like a great girl, I'm glad you have her," Marie said, looking at me, then looking back towards Robbie. "I'm glad you both have her."

"Thanks, Mum, she's my whole world," I muttered, feeling instantly sad and nostalgic about the three of us spending any time together.

She looked up at me with hope in her eyes. I wanted to get out of there before the tears I saw pooling in her eyes spilled. I nodded once, then walked away and back into the truck to go get my girl a burger.

Epilogue

Rosie

"Hey, baby, and hey, baby," Ben called as he arrived home from work.

It had been six weeks since we'd found out we were expecting and he was on a complete high—we both were. Ben was on cloud nine; actually, screw cloud nine, it was more like cloud fifteen. I had never seen him this overjoyed and excited. It warmed my heart when I thought about him being a dad.

He'd spent the last two weeks tending to my every need, adamant he was going to keep me positive and happy. He had read a book that said that a baby's happiness started in the womb, and he was obsessed. It was very out of character to see him singing to my stomach.

Everyone else was so excited for our news. Rachel had started sending me over baby items via a courier. A beautiful pram-style pushchair had arrived that had belonged to Freddie and Bella. Ben had practised putting it up and taking it down repeatedly and even made me practise too. Yawning, I watched him demonstrate to me, Billy and Robbie how to put it into my truck for the fifth time that hour.

How incredibly lucky I felt in that moment, watching three especially important people acting very seriously over the pushchair that would carry around the most important member of our family.

Life was different, life was better. I finally felt like I was really living.

Ben

It had been over a year since I'd first seen those bright green eyes on that ferry and life had changed for the better.

Now I watched with a proud smile as Rosie introduced our beautiful baby girl to our friends and family. Moments like this, I was able to appreciate how many amazing people we had around us. I beamed from ear to ear, my eyes not moving from where my girl was carrying our baby through the crowd.

She stood up by the bar of the Swan. The bunting had been changed to pink, mixing in with the 'Welcome to the world' signs that Miranda had spent time hanging in preparation for today. There were so many people in the room I loved and cared about, but my eyes didn't move from Rosie's.

"Go on then, don't leave us in suspense, what did you call her? Did you go with any of my suggestions?" Trent cheered, playing to the crowd as usual.

"For the seventeenth time, they obviously weren't going to call her Trentianna." Miranda scowled from beside him as she lifted her mojito to her lips.

Rosie laughed, then cleared her throat, all eyes focused on her. "We've decided to call her Sofia." Her eyes hesitantly flicked to my mine, then in the direction of Robbie where he was sat beside our mum. We'd both known we wanted to name her after my sister—we had spoken to Robbie previously about this, but decided to leave it as a surprise for my mum.

I heard her loud sniff before she barrelled into me. My mum and I had come a long way since that ugly moment in the restaurant. Rosie had been instrumental in bringing us together and building a family around our baby.

"To baby Sofia!" Rachel lifted her glass above her head, Bella balanced on her other hip.

Rosie made it through the small crowd and headed straight for me. I wrapped my arms around both my girls and held them close. She leant back and looked up into my eyes, lifting her glass of water to meet mine. "To knowing it may take time, but it really will get better." With a small smile she went to drink to our private cheers.

Placing a finger on her glass, I stopped her from taking a sip and clinked my glass against hers. "To happily ever afters."

Printed in Great Britain
by Amazon

23206617R00128